SINS

OF THE

FATHERS

A BREWSTER COUNTY NOVEL

NASH BLACK

IF Publishing
Jamestown, Kentucky

Sins of the Fathers
A Brewster County Novel
All Rights Reserved
Copyright © 2007 Nash Black
V3.0 R1.1

Cover Image © 2007 JupiterImages Corporation
All Rights Reserved. Used With Permission.

IF Publishing
Jamestown, Kentucky

ISBN-13: 978-1-4327-0724-8

Printed in the United States of America

DEDICATION

To the Lake Cumberland Children's Advocacy Center

CHARACTERS

Brewster County – an area of Kentucky enclosed, by the Cumberland, Kentucky, Mississippi, Ohio, and Tennessee Rivers.

Elton Fightmaster – lawyer who assumed his father's law practice when his father died.

Marcy Lane – screen name Marci Layne, high school classmate of Elton

Philip Andrews – insurance agent, high school classmate of Elton and Marcy

Jobi Andrews – younger sister of Philip Andrews, married to Bill Leighton

Bill Leighton – assistant to president of the bank, high school classmate of Elton, Marcy and Philip

Dan Sommers – sheriff of Brewster County

Gilbert Harrington, Prosecuting County Attorney

Silas Morgan – Circuit Court Judge – presides at the trial

Tom Clement – owner and publisher of the Brewster County Banner

Cadel Beckworth – president of First Farmer's Bank and Trust Co.

Elroy Mason Harris – local handyman
Lon Chambers – local handyman
James Bryan Stanley – priest
Benjamin Lehman – rabbi
All four men served together in the WWII and are close friends

Robert "Wilson" Curtis Wilson – master chef

Various other Brewster County residents

PROLOGUE

May 1955

Locker-doors slam inside my head. The warning bell sounded, but a pack of snotty seniors block the hall. They're making fun of me and my frizzy hair.

They're planning a party. I know because I listened to my brother, Philip, making plans on the phone. He said it was only for seniors. They never include me—like my Daddy does.

I'm invisible. Jobi Andrews doesn't exist when, he's with his friends. He doesn't want anyone to know Miss Kinky Top is his sister.

We peons have to squeeze around them or be late for class. They don't know I'm watching. They don't know I'm alive. Marcy Lane can have that stupid Elton who's always hanging around her. Bill Leighton is mine. I love Bill.

Icky Elton Fightmaster bends down like a lost scarecrow to pick up Marcy Lane's notebook. She dropped it on purpose to give the boys a peek down her blouse when she stooped.

They bump heads. He's a klutz. A foot taller than

anyone else—wears that ugly shoe with a brace. It always gets in the way. His head got in the way this time when he came down from the clouds. Serves them both right to look like knock-heads.

Bill. I saw him! He put his hand on her butt. How can he touch that flashy piece of trash? Her own father didn't want her. He dumped her on her aunt and took off to the army.

It is easy to see them in the mirror on my locker door. I look like a freak. I'm trying to tug a comb through my hair. It hurts. Callie Rogers gave me a Toni perm last night. It didn't come out like the picture on the box. I look like Prissy in *Gone With the Wind*. Mother made me come to school. I hate her.

I sent Bill a note. I stuck it through the vent in his locker. He wadded it up and threw it in the garbage can. He hangs around Marcy Lane with her brassy hair and big boobs, ignoring me. She looks like a cow that needs milking.

I can tell Mother about the party. Daddy will raise the roof if he knew Philip was going out drinking after graduation. He won't let him have his car. It'd serve Philip right for snubbing me. Big senior, some splash with no wheels; that would fix Mr. Thinks He's Big.

No. I've got a better idea. Callie. Callie loves a party. We'll take her father's car and follow them.

My Daddy has a bottle under the sink in the kitchen. Mother said it was cleaning fluid, but I know better. I saw him drink it after Mother said we shouldn't make him mad. You can't drink cleaning fluid.

She's always saying, "Don't make your father mad." She's the one. I listen at night when they think I'm asleep.

Philip sleeps with a pillow over his head. I watch him

through the crack in the door, when he comes down the hall at night. He doesn't sleep in pj's.

Daddy doesn't make enough money. Mother gets furious when I ask for high heels or a lipstick. She says we are going to the poor house because of my wants. She was really pissed when she found out I got the money out of her purse for the Toni.

That's why she made me come to school. To show me up for taking the money. She told me my hair will fall out because it's burned. I'll hide in the restroom until after school, then no one will see my hair.

My Daddy won't see it in the dark. He sees me, the real me. I'm his little love, not ole hateful. I try—he doesn't hit me like he does Mother when they're yelling.

I'll get the bottle to take to the party. They won't make us go home if we have booze. We'll need to take a blanket.

I'll wear my new sun dress. I got it special for Bill. It makes me look bigger in the chest. My Daddy gave me the money. He likes for me to have pretties. Mother says I'm too young to wear a bra but I have a Merry Widow. I'll use her girdle and the helpers from the mail order house. I'll look super.

My hair isn't blonde. It's not even brown. Mother won't let me use peroxide; only tramps use it. Now it's all frowzy. Callie ruined my hair, but in the dark Bill won't see it.

* * * * *

"Who was that?" Callie jerks the wheel, making the tires bump off the road. She's a terrible driver.

"I don't know. The headlights were in my eyes." She can ask some of the dumbest questions. Who cares?

"Are you sure your brother knows we're coming to the party? Papa didn't want me driving after dark. You know I don't have a license."

"I told you. I want to surprise them. See—right there in the drive to the old Hutchins' place. There's my Daddy's car. Pull in behind it."

I can see the red and white Chevy convertible Bill got for graduation in front of my Daddy's Ford. My Bill is here, waiting for me.

"Come on. I know where they are. There's an old log cabin near the creek. Hurry up. We'll miss the fun."

"It's dark out here. I can't see."

"Hush, Callie. Do you want them to hear us and spoil the surprise? I have a bottle. They'll love us for bringing it. I know the way. See—you can see. The moon is coming out from behind the clouds."

"A full moon, perfect! Let go of my arm. You'll cause me to trip." I whisper to her but she keeps her fingers clamped like a leech.

"Does your Mother know you borrowed her shoes?"

Questions—questions, Callie is always asking stupid questions. "Sure, I do it all the time. They're tight, but sling pumps have to be to stay on. I'll get a pair of my own for my birthday." My Daddy will get them for me, no matter what Mother says. He always gets nice things for me. I'm his little love.

I head straight for a beam of light, near the old cabin.

"Ouch! We're in blackberry bushes. You got off the path."

"Keep quiet. Let's get close and listen," I hiss at the silly fool. It's so still.

Doesn't sound like much of a party? I can't hear the portable radio I gave Philip for graduation. He put it in

Daddy's car before supper.

He told me it was super. Mr. Carstairs was busy hanging the new sign when I got it. He didn't see me.

I grab Callie's skirt to keep her from walking into the clearing. She's so dense.

Goofy Elton isn't here but I can see Philip and Bill. Philip is holding a flashlight. They're looking at a lump on the ground. I'd recognize that brassy red hair anywhere, it's Marcy Lane. Bill is squatting beside it, he reaches out and touches it. . .ugh. His shirt is torn, like he caught it on a blackberry bush or tripped over a stump in the dark.

"She's not breathing. She's dead." His voice is flat. I have to strain to hear him.

"Dead! Bill, she can't be. You got here before me." Philip's voice squeaks. He tries to keep it deep, but it changes when he gets excited. It makes him so mad he gets red in the face. Only girls blush; it looks dopey on boys. I practice blushing in the bathroom mirror so I can look demure.

Callie lets out a screech. I kick her hard, which hurts my toes. Philip turns the big flashlight toward us and shines the beam in our faces. I can't see.

"My God! It's your bratty sister and Callie Rogers." Bill shouts at Philip. "How did they get here?"

Philip drops the flashlight. It lands on Marcy Lane, who's curled in a ball. There are dark spots on her crinolines. She doesn't have on any panties. I knew she was a cheap whore. She looks, much better—dead. My Bill said she was dead! Good riddance; now Bill will love me.

Featherbrained Callie starts blubbering; she's acting the fool. She plops down on the ground. Doesn't she know she's wrinkling her skirt? She'll get grass stains on it, like the lump has.

Philip yells at me, "You're snooping, again."

"Don't you talk to me like that, Philip Andrews. I'll tell Mother what you're doing out here."

"Button your lips. Can't you see we got problems? Real problems."

"Oh, that—dump it in the old root cellar. Tom Clement told Elton they're going to bulldoze the whole place, on Saturday, for cottages. I heard him. No one will ever find it."

"We can't do. . . ."

"Of course you can. You don't want people to know you were with her when she died. How will you explain to Miss Cynthia? What will she think?" I can feel their eyes drilling holes in me. I must keep talking so they won't know I'm scared. I've never seen a corpse.

"Look. I heard Miss Cynthia tell Mother at church last Sunday that Marcy wants to go to Capital City after graduation. Miss Cynthia doesn't approve of nice girls leaving home before they get married. When they do, they become tramps." I put my hands on my waist so Bill will see how nice I'm built. Better than any dead slut.

"Shut up. All you ever do is sneak around listening. You're a regular snooper."

Callie keeps whimpering, not being an ounce of help. Silly idiot.

"Get them out of here. I know where the root cellar is. Remember? We played pirates there." Bill sounds disgusted with Callie. "Take them back to the car. I'll meet you in town."

Philip grabs my arm and pulls Callie to her feet. He pushes us up the path. He's mad. I can hear him grinding his teeth.

I shaved my legs using my Daddy's razor. Blackberry

bushes snag my new nylons. It took forever to get the seams straight. Now Philip has ruined them. I'll have to get another pair at the drugstore; when no one is looking.

Callie is blubbering and hiccuping at the same time. She sounds so funny. "She's dead. We shouldn't leave her. It's not right."

Philip puts his arm around her, but jabs me in the back to keep walking. He never pays attention to me. I whisper to her, "Can it. You sound stupid. Blow your nose. You're snuffling."

Philip hears me and pinches my arm. I kick at him and almost fall. My ankle hurts but he keeps pushing. My Daddy will take a strap to him for hurting me.

I call around Phillip to Bill, "Catch up with us after you go home to change your shirt. You got it all dirty. We're going to Hamilton's Drug store for a soda."

He turns his back to Marcy and looks off into the woods. He can't stand the sight of the lump, either. He'll get his hands filthy moving it.

Philip gives me another hard poke; wait till we get home. I'll make him sorry he's mean to me.

Going to the drugstore is perfect. I can pull off my ruined nylons in the car. My full skirt will hide my bare legs. They look like I have on hose. Callie and I sit out in the sun with iodine mixed in baby oil on our legs.

The crowd will think Philip and Callie are together and Bill's my date. He'll notice me. He'll love me like my Daddy.

"Hurry—everybody will be gone. She wasn't one of us."

* * * * *

They're fighting again. Mother is yelling at my Daddy. Philip and Bill are at the university. They've been gone a long time. I didn't have anything to do with Marcy's accident. Why should I care? Philip says I have no feelings. Yes, I do. I love Bill.

I told Marcy's aunt I saw her talking to a drummer in front of the hotel, the night of graduation. Callie just stood there, but Miss Cynthia thought she was telling the story too.

They cleared and plowed over the old root cellar. Now there are cute little cabins scattered through the woods. It's funny to think of her squished under one of those cabins.

I try to sleep with the pillow over my head the way Philip does. I can still hear them. Mother is making my Daddy mad. I crawl out of bed so they won't hear me and peek through the crack in the door to see what she's doing to my Daddy.

She's making my head hurt. My Daddy will be mad if she hurts me! She's screaming at my Daddy.

"I cleaned my car. Marcy Lane's purse and a pair of panties were under the front seat. I found a pair of ruined nylon stockings under the floor mat in your car. You've been screwing a girl who's the same age as your son. How dare you?"

I can't stand it when Mother screeches at my Daddy. I'll make her stop. I yank open the door and plunge into the dark hall. I put my hands out so I won't bump into the cedar wardrobe yelling at her as I run down the hall.

"No! It was Philip! Philip was with her. My Daddy wouldn't do that. He wouldn't touch that slut. He loves me." I push her away from my Daddy.

Dry wood snaps and cracks as it does when you break a stick for a camp fire. The banister moves as I shove. The silky smooth satin of her gown slides through my fingers. Her scream tears the cloth as small piece clings to my hand.

I look over the edge, her head is sideways and the red floor runner is scrunched around her. I let go of the rag and watch it slowly flutter down in the glow from the candle shaped hall light. It drifts to one side and then floats back toward her as if it is trying to find the place it tore from her gown. I can't wear her night-slip again. It's ruined!

My Daddy's hands feel so warm, rubbing my shoulder. He is whispering soft pretties to me. It serves her right for making my Daddy mad. . .saying he was with Marcy Lane when I'm his little love. She won't scream at my Daddy anymore, and say bad things. I hate her.

He pulls me back from the broken banister and carries me to bed.

"Go to sleep, my little love. You had a bad dream." My Daddy holds me. He loves me. He won't leave me. His hands are so soft as he strokes me. I'm his little love.

* * * * *

The settling boards creak in the dark places of our old house as if a ghost is walking down the stairs. I shiver in my bed and strain to listen. A muffled crack followed by thunder like the boom of Granddad's shotgun, invades the silence.

It's the same sound as when I go hunting with my Daddy. He won't take Philip because he flinches when he pulls the trigger. One time he pulled both triggers at the same time. The kick knocked him flat on his behind. I laughed because I knew my Daddy wouldn't let Philip pinch me.

Maybe he'll take me hunting tomorrow. She won't be here to say I must go to school. He tucked the covers under my chin and kissed me before he left. My Daddy loves me.

I'm his little love.

The boom was far away. It's cold without my Daddy. I'll go to him.

Bill will be home next week. I got him to promise to take me to the drugstore for a soda. He's mine. I can give him every thing she did. I know how; my Daddy taught me.

CHAPTER 1

November 1968

I am humming *Whenever I Feel Afraid* as I climb the steps to the verandah of the Wren Hotel. I am happy, and it is a catchy tune. The long weeks in Capital City are behind me—no more hospitals.

The square is peaceful when I glance back where the shadows thicken under the old trees in the amber glow of the street lights. I am alive and walking free from pain; I have no right to be as lucky as I am.

I lift my left leg high over the threshold, treading carefully to avoid the worn carpeting inside the door. The doormat has been moved and the threadbare snags are treacherous if the brace under my shoe should catch a loop of pile. My new brace is made of aluminum, so light I can barely feel the weight. It is not noticeable unless someone looks for it.

The doctor in Capital City believes I can eventually leave it off altogether, with constant exercise and another

1

series of operations. Do I have the strength to endure those long weeks of recuperation? So easy to say yes and so difficult to admit I am a fool to believe in miracles.

I wear my khakis long. Bell-bottoms flair over the brace and the top of my shoe so I do not catch my heel on the hem. I have to order my trousers tailor-made; the ones off the rack come just past my knees.

The special in the dining room is pot roast, their only decent evening meal. Fried chicken is reserved for Sunday dinner. I hate to cook for myself. The hospital food assaulted my taste buds, but tonight I have high hopes.

Betty Clement invites me to join them on a Saturday night when she tests the recipes for the next issue of the *Banner*. I am delighted to oblige. She is a fine cook even if her numerous girl friends do happen to stop by for a visit.

I am onto her attempts to find me a wife. Some have developed into friendships, but I have never found a special girl to replace the one I lost. There is not any sense in kidding myself. I cannot lose what was never mine.

As I enter the dining room, I pause and take a deep breath of home. After a month in the hospital, with its prevailing stink of antiseptic cleaning fluids, the low-lying cigar-smoke in the lobby smells wonderful. The sharp aroma of onions and grease hangs heavy in the air. They are balanced by the crisp scent of Pine Sol. The same odors I have inhaled all my life.

The three residents who have permanent rooms in the hotel are in their self-assigned places: along the windows looking out over the square so they can see who is coming to supper. They have watched me amble across the square without the least change of expression on their faces.

My gaze drifts—stops hard. Breath is sucked from my lungs.

I am eight years old and looking into the brilliant green

eyes of the new girl Miss Stephenson has told to carry my books so I can use my crutches. Undying love is born on the heady perfume of chalk dust. The same flame-burnished hair glows around the famous face. I have watched her for hours from the dark movie house in Cloverton.

I dream I am Fred Astaire and can whisk her away on clouds of moonlight, dancing from star to star. I can ride up on a great white stallion, bend down and lift her to safety, then canter into the sunset.

She smiles. No one has informed my left leg aluminum will not respond to her powerful magnetic force. I clasp the back of a chair as I begin to fold and fall against the table. She waits for me to get my feet in their proper place, as she had so many times. She never tried to help, just paused until I righted things for myself.

I ignore the eyes of the diners burning a hole in my back and their indulgent smiles. I return her smile with a self-deprecating grin and stumble toward my destiny on trembling legs.

It is an extravagant gesture but when she extends her hand I raise it to my lips. "Will you marry me?"

"No." Her face is serious and still.

I laugh, but my heart has stopped beating. "Marcy, it is wonderful to see you. Is your aunt sick? I have been out of town, I just got back."

"She's fine, Elton; you know Aunt Cynthia, she'll live forever. Sit down. My neck is getting cramped looking up at you." She retrieves her hand and covers the place where I kissed it with the other hand. She is not wearing a wedding ring.

If Miss Cynthia is fine, why is Marcy here in Brewster County? I was positive she would never return.

I must stop staring, but she is so beautiful. Hidden away in my bedroom is every magazine that has carried her picture on the cover. I have two billboard posters from the movie house in Cloverton. The ultimate moviefan who worships with fevered devotion.

Even to myself, I sound like a rube. I am a county lawyer. The waitress sets the Chinese love-story grill plate containing the evening's special and a mug of coffee in front of me. My fork is a foreign object that I have forgotten how to use. I notice her plate; she is not eating either, globules of fat from the roast are congealing around the edge of the rim.

"Elton, you are the best person in Clydsville to have as a dinner partner."

"When did you get home?" We both ask the same question at the same time and then laugh because our answers are the same.

"This afternoon."

She obviously knows about the hospital and brushes the gory details aside. Her eyes spare my pride and convey a deep knowledge of my pain. She lost her little girl in a horrible miscarriage of fortune. I have read every newspaper report and fan magazine article of her tragedy. But those eyes compel me not to open the door. We honor each other's pain with a lift of the heavy water glasses.

The waitress can barely restrain herself from begging for an autograph from the famous movie star, Marci Layne, as she refills our mugs. I am content to bask in the glow of the only love of my life.

"Do you remember how Murtle Clayton would tell stories of the drummers who could never hit the slopjar? She had to scrub the walls where the men missed." Marcy looks at me, her eyes shimmering with laughter, her head tilted slightly to the left. The celluloid copy could never catch their depths.

"Yes." I can feel my ears start to burn. How like Marcy, bringing up an absurd subject, to confuse and delight the listener.

"It's true! They haven't even replaced the wallpaper. My room smells like years of stale urine. In the corner the paper has been scrubbed clean of the pattern, but the thunder mugs are gone. Two rooms now share a bath; so I rented two rooms to have a suite." She giggles and pushes her mashed potatoes around on the plate before talking a small bite. Miss Cynthia never allowed anyone to play with their food. Her look holds the mischief of a naughty child who is indulging her most guilty desire.

"No other place knows how to make light and fluffy mashed potatoes with real cream and butter, but here in Brewster County. I know. I've tried them all over the world, only to be disappointed. They never taste the same."

She reaches across the table and covers my hand with hers. "No, Elton, don't ask. I'll come by your office in a few days to discuss business. Just for tonight, we are two friends back in town having. . . . "

Her hand pushes down on mine hard and I hear, for the first time, footsteps, behind me. Marcy's mobile face drains of color, but her lips ease into a bland semblance of the smile. "Hello, Bill."

I look up, though I know who stands by our table. Her hand retreats into her lap.

"Marcy, I just want to say how glad we are you've come home. I heard at the bank, just a few minutes after you registered."

Marcy's foot is on mine, preventing me from standing.

A strident, demanding voice pierces the quiet between

two people who are searching for what to say next.

"Bill, we have guests." His wife pulls his arm up and pushes herself under it, placing his hand on her hip. "Bill and I are married. We have a son. We'll leave you to the dessert. They're having chocolate pie, but from seeing your last picture, you don't need extra sweets. Cameras always tell the truth."

Bill's face assumes a distant expression. He disappears into himself when she crosses the boundary of civility. He is ashamed, but rather than make a scene he turns and walks away, dragging her while she struggles to keep his hand on her hip. He didn't even say good night.

I cannot remember her as rude as she has just been to both Bill and Marcy, but there is no understanding Jobi Andrews Leighton.

She is Philip's sister and has always been strange. Maybe she had been drinking before they came to the hotel? The story is whispered around that her mother kept a bottle hidden under the kitchen sink—Hank Sidmore's stuff.

Maud Tosh waves from across the room as Rupert frowns. I acknowledge their presence. Maud genuinely loves people but Rupert, like Jobi Leighton, is very possessive of his spouse. I have no desire to invite them to join us. I want Marcy to myself.

I turn to her to apologize for Jobi as she says, "Elton, I've always known her. She doesn't interest me." Her fork flutters above her plate, but her knuckles are white.

"Bill disliked her when we were in school. She was always hanging around, listening to every word we said. He tolerated her because she was Philip's sister. I'm surprised he married her." She puts the fork on her plate and props her chin in her hands. "I didn't know."

"They married after he finished college. He went to work at the bank. Philip could not control her after their parents died. No one knew they were dating. Three years ago, little Bill was born. They live in the Anderson home, though you would not recognize it. Jobi had the house remodeled.

"I am on the board at the bank. Cadel Beckworth, the president, did not want to make the loan. Philip may have helped them. I do not know."

"How is Philip?"

"Philip sells insurance. He seldom goes near the bank and never has much to say. I do not think he has gotten over his parents' death. He never finished school. It bothers me we are no longer friends, but I guess being away at school does that to cliques."

"What's that old song? It has the line, 'Those wedding bells are breaking up that old gang of mine.'"

"Maybe; Philip is not married. I was feeling sorry for myself, though I did expect them to stop by to say hello when I took over my father's office. Philip and Bill were pallbearers for his funeral, but drifted away, never even speaking to me.

"How is that for a small town gossip? You can get the real history if you have Callie Rogers do your hair. She has the beauty parlor across the square."

"Maybe, if I get desperate, but for now I think I will avoid getting marcelled, lavender-blue hair." She lets go her irrepressible laugh that tinkles like hundreds of tiny bells, and waves an expressive hand toward the window tables.

"No. I want to hear all the news about everyone from you. It will be the truth, not dressed up for the benefit of the movie star. You'll not try to make me feel like a failure because I don't have three children and. . .a husband." It is impossible not to hear the catch in her voice about the husband and child.

"Betty Clement tries matchmaking but she has given up or run out of candidates."

"Who is Betty Clement?"

"You remember Tom Clement?" She nods. "Betty is his wife. She is from Cloverton but has Brewster County connections. My sister married her brother before we graduated. Tom will want to interview you for the paper. Miss Cynthia can bring you up to date on the happenings in Clydsville."

She ignores my statement. "I'd rather hear it from the perspective of a contemporary. Now, tell all."

We start talking. At some point, the waitress removes our dinner plates, sets the chocolate meringue dessert down, and replaces the cold coffee mugs. We chatter with plenty of "do you remembers" and never notice the other diners leave the room.

I am unaware of anything but her smile. It will begin with a tiny quiver on the left of her mouth and flow across her pink lips, which are devoid of lipstick. Someone blinks the lights because they want to close and go home. I have no choice but to let her go.

Marci Layne, the star, climbs the stairs and follows the corridor without looking back. Her dress of diagonal multi-colored stripes that meet in the center of the back and front make her appear taller than five feet. The skirt barely brushes her knees, falling free from her shoulders like a triangle. She turns and gives a brief wave before vanishing down the dimly lit hallway.

The peeling paint of the old hotel glistens and gleams like polished marble, while the globes below the ceiling-fans, filled with dead flies, glitter with the reflection of hundreds of glossy candles in elegant chandeliers.

A radio is playing the powerful sounds of WWL from New Orleans. The music duplicates the soft blues rhythm of her walk. I pick up the cane I purchased in Capital City from the umbrella stand by the front door. The feel of the dark walnut handle is warm in the palm of my hand as if the carved wood holds heat in its grooves.

The sweet smell of autumn clematis from Beatrice Carstairs' front porch drifts on the soft breeze as I start across the park. Stars shimmer in the navy-blue sky. I cannot dance like Gene Kelly through the streets of Paris, but I feel the regretful sigh of the nighthawk's lonely cry.

Marci Layne is home. The world responds to her magic as if touched by a wand. I can never want another woman as I desire her. It does not matter that she will not stay. Titania's spell is a dream of enchantment, and for however long, I am her willing prisoner, content to bask in her warmth. A vision from the silver screen has come down to earth and is mine for an evening. Time has no significance.

CHAPTER 2

I see you saved my seat. Did you spend the night or am I horning in on a date?"

"You are being ridiculous."

Tom Clement pulls out his chair, sits down and props his elbows on the table. "Some crowd, wearing Sunday suits on a Thursday. Looks as if word of your evening has made the wires."

The dining room is packed. The only time it is this crowded is when the Wren hosts the St. John's Day breakfast for the Masons.

"Check your pockets. You forgot to remove the moth balls from your father's jacket."

"I'm a reporter. Think I should get a porkpie hat with a card saying press stuck in the band?" His steel-grey eyes gleam like polished silver as he pulls a small brown notebook and a pencil stub from his pocket.

"That bilious green bow tie is a hallmark of bad taste. I am surprised Betty let you out the front door."

"For implying I would let my wife dictate what I should wear when I am working, you will have to look at this tie every morning for the rest of your life. Now, tell me about your night at the cinema." He holds the pencil poised above the pad as a frantic waitress sets a plate of slightly scorched scrambled eggs in front of him.

"Where are my coffee, bacon and biscuits?"

"Sorry, Mr. Clement. We've run out, Sam has some biscuits in the oven. I'll bring them in just a minute." She hurries away before he can start complaining. Tom would never utter a cuss word, he uses four syllable ones with great style.

"Tom, I told Marcy you would want an interview. She did not refuse but she will not be here for breakfast, so stop breaking your neck looking over your shoulder."

"Flown the coop because of the reception committee?"

"Maybe, but she was tired. Yesterday, she drove from Kansas City, Missouri. Now may we change the subject? Did the elections go to suit you?"

The waitress delivers his breakfast and refills my coffee.

"Nixon's a crook." He mumbles around a bite of biscuit.

"I was referring to the big upset."

"Gilbert Harrington pushing out Victor Davis?"

"Yes. Mr. Davis has been County Attorney for what, twenty years or more?"

"To be exact, twenty-three years."

"What happened?"

"Elton, people are tired of watching the news and seeing someone famous shot on a balcony or in a kitchen.

"Tired of getting the paper out of their mail box and reading someone who attends their church has been indicted.

"Tired of poor prices for the crops they've nursed through floods, drought, worn-out soil, and mold on tobacco before it gets to the barn.

"Tired of some snot-nosed kid fresh out of the university

telling them what they've been doing all of their lives is wrong when the preacher tells them the same thing every Sunday.

"Tired of every time they turn around someone has their hand out wanting a donation for some worthy cause when they still have not found a cure for the common cold.

"Tired of attending the funeral of a kid down the block who played with their children. Tired of being scared the next one may be theirs and ashamed of being thankful today is not their day."

"I asked about Davis and you give me an editorial."

"While you were in the hospital Harrington got busy. He visited every house on every road in the county. He promised no special favors for the rich from the prosecutor's office. Do you know of any in Brewster County?"

"Any what?"

"Rich people."

"Only ones I ever heard of were the Curtis and Laurence families who owned the mines, but the mines were closed after the first world war."

Tom waves his knife. "People believe if a guy has a dime more than they do, then he's rich. Even churches teach that if a man is rich heaven doesn't have a place for him. Remember the parable, 'It is easier for a camel to go through the eye of a needle than for a rich man to enter Heaven.'

"He used envy and mistrust to sway the voters with platitudes they have heard all their lives but never examined for validity. I could not catch him telling an outright lie. Trying to explain the difference would have every money-grubbing sanctimonious preacher in the county canceling their subscriptions."

"You are ruining my digestion. You have also heard all your life, you never discuss religion or politics at the table." I cannot resist teasing him when he gets in a crusading mode, but Tom is skeptical of the motives of anyone who indulges in generalizations and stereotypes.

"When you worry about the paper's circulation, which shoe are you trying to fit?"

He laughs, "You got me there, but mark my words, Harrington has his eye on Capital City. He wants to be state attorney general, maybe even governor. We're only a stepping stone for his vaunted ambition. People swallowed his hogwash, so for the next four years we are stuck with the pompous ignoramus.

"The people know the only election where their vote makes a difference is the home ballot. No one will admit voting for him, but someone did. Davis controlled the cemetery vote.

"They want to go back to a world they think was safe and peaceful. They don't remember how many funerals their parents and grandparents attended when whole families died of diseases they've never heard of. Funerals weren't even funerals, bodies were wrapped in a blanket and taken out to the back pasture and buried, then the living got on with it."

"I assume you are not enamored with the voting public."

"We have a serious problem at the courthouse." He drops money on the check. "Before you make me forget, Betty said come to supper Saturday night and bring a friend."

He stalks from the dining room writing furiously on the pad. Tom Clement on a new crusade. The *Banner* will be interesting to read next week.

CHAPTER 3

Do you draw up deeds?"

I did not hear the stranger's approach. It is Wednesday afternoon and I am in my grandfather's rocker on the front porch reading the *Banner*. This is a ritual in small towns, when everyone closes up shop for a break in the middle of the week. His face is as familiar as Cary Grant's, but I cannot put a name to it. Tall, close to my height, about six foot three or four. I would not have to look down at him if I were to stand.

"Yes, I am a lawyer, but I have a previous appointment for this afternoon." I am going horseback-riding with Marcy. This is the first time I can say with pride that I have other plans.

Tall handsome stranger, and Marcy in town. I feel jealous of the carefully trimmed black hair, and the changeable hazel eyes that glint with humor as I study him. Instinctively, I distrust this man because I know he has a power to attract that will leave me outside, gazing in a window. His wide mouth crinkles into a slight grin.

"Elton, I grew eight inches after I left school. You don't

remember me, I'm Clayton Forrester."

"Clayton Forrester! But you died—in Korea."

"No. . .not so I noticed. Where did you hear that piece of misinformation?"

I carefully fold the paper, hiding Marcy's picture as I lay it across my lap. "I attended your funeral. They closed school; we all went."

He abruptly sits down on the top step of the porch and puts his head in his hands. "My grandmother?"

He is asking a question; his concern is for the woman who reared him. "She was there and very proud. It was a military funeral for an honored hero. The American Legion staged their full service for the first active soldier to be laid to rest since the big war. She buried your Purple Heart with the body. The grave is in the service section, between your father and great-grandfather."

He looks up to where I am sitting in the cane rocker. A rueful half smile lights his face as he studies me. Glints of gold flecks on a hazel sea scrutinize my face with bewildered intensity. I can see the admired upper classman in the grown man. His stare reduces me to freshman status.

"I guess that makes twice Grams was proud of me." He is talking slowly, but I am not sure he is speaking to me; there is distance in his vibrant voice.

"She fought like hell to make sure I finished high school—the first one in our family. She saved coupons and refund checks to order a new dress from Montgomery Ward for my graduation. The building of the lake and the loss of her land took her pride. I knew she was dead, so I didn't come back when I could; I'd had enough pain.

"Can't evict a corpse. What am I going to do?"

Clayton, like Marcy, makes no move to help me as I slowly get to my feet, flexing a leg gone stiff. I open the door for him, ashamed of my jealousy.

"Come in. Now that I am over the shock of seeing a ghost I will see if I can find us a beer." It is hard for me to accept two people I never thought would return to Brewster County in less than a week.

"Is it legal?"

"Is what? The beer? Of course; I brought it when I was in Capital City. I will not keep Hank Sidmore's rotgut in the house. Let's go in the kitchen, it is more comfortable than my office." It also faces my mother's walled garden, which is very private.

Clayton ignores the glass I offer. He picks up the bottle and takes a deep swallow, clearly disturbed. What a mix-up, to come home to find you are dead and buried.

"I don't mean to be rude, Elton, but I have to think." He picks up the bottle and walks out into the garden, which I try to keep in some semblance of control, but the beds are overgrown from neglect. I watch him pace the narrow paths and I cannot remember ever feeling as sorry for anyone. When he makes a circuit by the back door, I notice a jagged scar that runs from behind his left ear down into his shirt.

Eighteen years is a long time; where has he been? His clothes do not have the appearance of off-the-rack wear. His hands, when he grasped the bottle, were soft, with carefully trimmed nails. The deep tan shows he spends time outdoors.

His walk is hesitant, like mine when the pain becomes difficult. He returns slowly to the house.

"I came back to buy a vacation place. I wanted it on or near the lake. Even though I don't have family here anymore, these hills and valleys are a part of me. Late at night if I'm not working on a project, I remember the breaking rays coming up across the river. I can hear the croak of the frogs or the rustle of leaves as a fox passes along the bank. My grandmother claimed I had Cumberland River water for blood, and I'm not sure she wasn't right."

"Clayton, the river, and now the lake are our heritage. I enjoy driving down some of the old ferry roads listening to the night."

"As I drove around the square, I remembered your father was a lawyer. I saw you sitting on the porch reading the paper. That hasn't changed. I don't need a calendar to tell me it's Wednesday afternoon."

"What are you going to do?"

"Elton, I have no idea. Would it make a difference if I went out in the street and shouted, 'Hey, there's been a mistake? Look at me; I'm alive.' My life isn't here, nor is it ever likely to be, except for fishing and hunting."

His right hand snaps to a salute. He tilts his bottle toward my glass and we click a silent toast to our own unknown soldier buried so far from home. "Rest in peace, whoever you are.

"I got mine at Kumsong, the last Chinese offensive. We were taking a banging from their mortar fire. Some Turks pulled me out and I got separated from my unit. I guess someone identified a mangled body as mine. I have no idea. It's ancient history."

"I have an idea that may keep the ladies of the Legion Auxiliary from rustling their bustles. You could buy a place in another county.

"You could pick up a small property or even the back of an old farm. No one would recognize your name, as it would not have the significance it does in Brewster County."

"Elton," Clayton asks as he drops onto a chair by the

table, "have you spent your life solving other people's problems?"

I laugh, a comfortable feeling. I like Clayton. "I have never heard it expressed in that manner but solving problems is what lawyers do. I will be more than happy to fix a deed for you when you find the right place."

"It'll be interesting to spend my visit incognito. I'll take my time and look around until I find what I want, as you suggest, in another county. Are Elroy Harris and Lon Chambers still around?"

"Yes, Lon built a pair of houseboats on the river for them, just after the lake was impounded, from old logs they fished out of the river."

Clayton looks sharply at me and starts laughing. "I know where they discovered them, south of where Lost Man Creek enters the river there is a big deep cove."

I take a sip of my beer to cover my surprise. "Right, that is where they are parked. The houseboats are pulled in close to the bank so they are not caught in the rough current when the dam is generating. How did you know?"

"I was with them the night they discovered the logs and damn near got myself killed. I imagine they intended to get rid of any potential competition. As a kid I wanted to run deliveries for Hank Sidmore. I pulled together an old '41 Ford from spare parts around the junkyards. Every minute I could slip off from my chores I'd follow them around."

I studied the man who had been the boy I had most wanted to emulate when we were in school. Carefully combed dark hair, light blue open-collared shirt and soft grey trousers, which are casual yet very expensive. It is hard to imagine this man wanting to work for Mr. Sidmore. He has an aura of danger. It is subtle, and has nothing to do with my desire to keep him away from Marcy.

I glance at the clock over the refrigerator. His eyes follow mine. Very little escapes him, as if the watchfulness is ingrained.

"What do you do?"

"Oh, I'm self-employed—much safer than my early ambitions. I was never as scared in Korea as I was the night I talked Elroy into letting me go on a run. Sheriff Daniels laid a trap and almost caught us. I was sitting in the back with all of those brown vinegar jugs in boxes—there wasn't any seat. I was bouncing around, trying to hold on. Those jugs were rolling and clanking. I kept trying to keep them from breaking." He takes a deep breath, shoots an eye toward the clock and grins at the memory.

"We hid the jugs in that old root cellar back of the Hutchins' place, where we played pirates as kids. Passed them down those rickety stairs. They hid their car in the back of a field, then they led me down that steep cliff in the dark to the river. The only thing I could see was the light square of the label where the straps crossed on Lon's bibs.

"We crawled through the willows and sycamore roots at the edge of the water; that's when we found the logs. I put my hand on a big snapper and screamed. Elroy pushed my head under, and one of those suckers rolled under us— over my leg—pinning me under water until Lon and Elroy rolled it off."

He is walking around the room, listening to the past, barely aware I am in the room.

"I never told anyone that story. They took me to my grandmother's and talked her into signing the papers so I could go in the service, same as my grandfather. She was against it because he never came home."

"Elroy learned motors in the big war, Lon was with him but I don't know how. Neither of them will say."

"They kept a stupid kid from getting himself killed trying to be a tough guy. Grams was a hard sell but she gave in with the stipulation I finish high school. I wish I could see them. . .only people still here I'd like to visit."

"Clayton, they keep secrets. They will be proud to talk to you. Elroy has a little garage out on Singleton Ferry Road when they are not working for Mr. Sidmore. Lon helps him in the shop."

We walk back to the front porch. I watch him drive out of my life in an E-Type Jaguar convertible. Whatever Clayton does, he never said, but it must pay, and he still loves classy, fast cars. My new Buick sedan sitting in the drive looks sedate and staid.

CHAPTER 4

"Ouch. Callie, you're pulling my hair."

"It's dry and brittle. You've got to give it a rest. I just colored it. You don't need another perm."

"It must be perfect. Marcy Lane is at the hotel. Bill is taking me to dinner in Cloverton."

"I know; Maud Tosh told me when she was in to have her comb-out. Marcy ate dinner at the hotel with Elton. Said they didn't know another soul was in the room. Do you think they have a case?" She wants to hear of a grand romance in the air.

"Elton. Don't be stupid. She was always after my Bill. I let her know. . .real fast: Bill is mine. I made sure his back was to her all evening."

"Jobi, of course Bill's yours; you've been married umpteen years."

"I wish she'd stayed dead."

"You do no such thing. I remember how thrilled I was when they ran that story in the *Banner* about how she'd made it in Hollywood."

"She never said a word and was only on the screen for a few minutes. Bill made me sit through that silly film twice while tears ran down his face. Imagine my embarrassment, the father of my child, Bill, crying in a movie."

"You're getting things mixed up. She made that first movie way before Little Bill was born, he's only three. I always wondered who found her after we left."

"Nobody found her, the old cow was faking. I told Philip but he didn't believe me. What are you doing? Give me that back!"

"Jobi, my customers like to read the magazines. You're tearing it to bits, it's the new one. What's wrong with you?"

Callie is always asking dumb questions. I don't want Bill to even see that bitch in a movie. I found that stupid article in his billfold and burned it. I saw how she took her hand away from Elton and looked at my Bill.

"If Bill is taking you to lunch? Where is Little Bill?"

"Emma Parker said she would watch him this morning while I get my hair done. What difference does it make? He's always over there anyway."

"She doesn't know you're going to be gone most of the afternoon and evening."

She said that to make me feel bad. She thinks I should stay home and fix supper for my men like they do on TV. Hot cookies for little Bill every day. I hate to cook—wish I could get a maid; my Daddy would have seen that I had a maid. Bill says we can't afford one.

"You can get an early start, since the bank will be closed this afternoon. I thought Bill played golf with Mr. Beckworth on Wednesday?"

"He does, silly. Cadel brings a friend and Calvin Forkes to make up the foursome with my Bill. I'm going to meet him at the country club for lunch before they tee off. He's going to teach me to play on Saturday.

"Move. You're standing in front of me. I can't see."

"Jobi, will you hold still while I finish these rollers. There is nothing on the square you haven't seen a hundred times. Bill is taking you to dinner and meeting you for lunch, that's wonderful. You don't need to worry about Marcy."

"There she is! She's coming down the steps of the hotel. I can see her flashy red hair. I'd never have that horrible color."

"Of course not, you're not a Lane; all the Lane's have red hair. I'm finished. Now get under the dryer. I've got a new *True Confessions*, which you love. Have a cigarette and watch the morning programs." Callie always keeps the shop television tuned to the stories so no one will miss an episode while their hair is drying.

"Callie! You know I don't smoke in public. Where's she going? Is she going to the bank?"

"So what if she is? You can't go out." Callie grabs my arm and pulls me back. It hurt; she hurt me.

"You've got curlers in your hair. Sit down." She bangs the hood over my head. "She is going to her car, the light-blue Lincoln convertible with California plates. It's parked behind the hotel."

I push up the dryer so I can hear her. She's as bad as the dentist who asks you questions with both hands in your mouth.

"Just look at your nails. You've been chewing them again. I'll give you a manicure while your hair dries."

"Where does she go every morning? She's been here a week. Miss Cynthia won't receive her."

"How do you know she won't? She is her blood-kin."

"I heard her tell Maud Tosh at church she'd never let Marcy in the house again after she took off with that salesman."

"But, Jobi! You told that fib."

"Don't but me. She never was anything but a tramp. She left with someone. . .who but a salesman?"

"Well, I never liked keeping secrets. It makes me feel creepy."

Callie pulls the dryer over my head and turns on the blower. I rode my bike out there after Philip was in bed and shoved a board against the door so her ghost couldn't get out. How did she get out of the root cellar?

* * * * *

Callie took so long to fix my hair I didn't add a tip when I signed the bill. I painted my nails with a second coat of Pink Passion while she was cutting Dan Sommers' hair. She can't sell a used bottle of polish, so I put it in my purse.

Marcy's convertible with the top down is parked where I always park by the front door of the clubhouse so I won't have to walk so far in dress shoes. Bill. . .my Bill is showing Marci Layne the golf club I gave him for Christmas. Those Hager Irons cost a fortune. How dare he even talk to that tramp. She's got on riding clothes, it's awful how skin tight they are. If she bends over, they'll split.

I ram the car between two trucks and hurry to get Bill's club out of her hands.

"You scraped the side of your car, Jobi. What are you doing here? Where's little Bill?"

"Did you forget? You're taking me to lunch."

"Jobi, I'm having lunch with Raymond Clark and the guys from the bank. We are going out to dinner. Where's little Bill?"

I give him a swift kick and pull the club from her hand. "Give me that. I gave it to Bill." What is she doing out here?

"Did you lose your horse?" I put the club back in Bill's bag, dusting off my gloves.

"Miss Layne, will you join us for lunch?"

I hadn't seen Cadel Beckworth come up behind me. Why is Cadel inviting her to our lunch? She keeps looking at my Bill, too dumb to say anything. Mr. Beckworth extends his arm to her. He is so polite, even to trash.

"Bill, put your bag by the door and we'll take these two lovely ladies to lunch."

"Marcy's got a date; she's dressed for riding. She wouldn't want to make the poor animal swaybacked by eating lunch." I force a smile and take Bill's arm. "Women aren't allowed in the club wearing pants."

The dumb cow looks at Mr. Beckworth, shamefaced for coming to the country club improperly dressed.

"Thank you for the invitation, but I'm meeting Elton to go riding."

She climbs into the blue car. The gall of her taking my parking place! I put my hand under Cadel's arm. Bill can't do a thing, but go with us into the clubhouse. She came out here to see my Bill but I got rid of her.

CHAPTER 5

Elton, you'll never guess what I just saw."

Marcy strides into my office as the front door slams. She is laughing so hard she bends over and clasps her hands on her knees.

"I give, what did you see?"

"Jobi. . .Jobi Leighton; she's crazy."

"Yes."

"I'm sorry, I shouldn't laugh, but it was so funny. I drove out to the country club to get a salad for lunch. Bill was there and was showing me his golf clubs. I was testing the swing when Jobi arrived.

"She scraped the side of a truck parking her car and left the door open in a rush to get between Bill and me. She was tottering in spike-heel sling pumps. They must have been four inches high, running—running across the gravel in those things."

"She does tend to overdress."

"Overdress. She was grotesque. Ruffles. Her dress had more ruffles than those outlandish costumes Carmen

Miranda wore. The skirt was so short it didn't cover her panty-girdle in the back. Her hat and gloves had ruffles, everything was a vile pink. She was wearing a wide brimmed-hat like the ones women wear to the Derby, perched on a beehive. It looked like a giant bird ready to take flight."

Her sentences sound as if they are punctuated with an exclamation marks. She is laughing but angry all at the same time. "Marcy, you are a threat to Jobi. She's fighting for possession."

"Elton, you sound small townish. Bill didn't expect her. He was waiting for his colleagues; they lunch and play golf on Wednesday afternoon. Let me sit down."

She sinks into a chair, laughter creasing the corners of her eyes. Beautifully tailored Marcy, dressed for riding in a dark green, long-sleeved silk shirt, twills, and well-worn boots. She has lost weight since they were made. The pants are gathered behind her gloves tucked under her belt. A green net holds her hair but little wisps escape to frame her face. Faint blue shadows tinge the skin under her eyes; Marcy is too thin.

"He kept asking about their son and wouldn't look at me when she yanked the club out of my hand. Cadel Beckworth saved the day. I got out fast, which reminds me, I didn't get a chance to eat."

"Want to go back to the country club?"

"She said women in pants weren't allowed in the club."

"For Marci Layne, the doyens will make an exception; besides, I hear they have a new chef."

"She's retired, but you're on. My car is behind yours if you don't mind the top down?"

CHAPTER 6

Elton is magnificent on a horse."

"Kathryn, I was sitting on the top rail of the paddock. His father kept shouting for him not to be a baby when his leg collapsed as he tried to mount a full-grown gelding. Elroy lifted him into the saddle and he did fine. Mr. Fightmaster was a cruel man; he pulled Elton off. He wouldn't tolerate Elroy coddling his son like his mother did.

"Lon Chambers brought out a Welsh pony. He stood there and backed Mr. Fightmaster down without saying a word. I was too young to understand what I was seeing but I've never forgotten that scene. We were in the fifth grade. Mr. Fightmaster left and never came back. After that, Elton's mother brought him out from town. She would pick me up to ride with him. It was a glorious summer.

"Lon taught him to mount from the right side like the Indians. He was so proud. I'd learned to ride on the Belgians at the farm, and between Elroy and Lon they managed to make fair riders of some rough prospects."

"I shouldn't intrude, but Elton is special. He worships you."

"Yes. He worships the illusion. He doesn't love the woman. Elton must have the illusions to endure what he faces in life. His friendship is much too vital to me to destroy it with a shoddy affair. He is one of the rare innocents of the world who make life precious.

"I've missed this view. I'd sit up here on my horse, a queen with her knights performing below on the great plain."

"You create illusions; don't hurt him. He doesn't know the difference."

"But I do. Who's that? He'll kill that horse."

"Philip Andrews, he's drunk. Come on, we'd better get down to your field of honor before John Henry loses his patience."

"Philip?"

* * * * *

"Elton, he was killing that horse. When did he start drinking?"

"Sometime after his parents died."

"When did that happen?"

I do not want to tell Marcy Philip's terrible story. I fumble with the cigarette lighter in the dash and light one I do not want. She deserves to know the truth. It had been hard for her to watch John Henry Burton pull him from the saddle while I held the bloody bridle to steady the trembling stallion.

Philip is not a mean drunk; he knew what he had done to that poor animal. He was in bad shape but the long walk back to the stables sobered him enough that he took the

29

reins from me and continued his walk.

Her face had been a tapestry of agony watching a grown man shamed before his friends. When we reached the stables, he disappeared into a tack room.

John Henry told us Philip would sleep it off before he let him drive back to town. When I looked in before we left, he was sprawled across a cot, dead to the world.

"After we started at the university. We shared a ground floor apartment, Bill, Philip and myself. I got permission to live off campus because of my leg.

"One night just before Thanksgiving Philip received a call from his father. His mother had fallen over the banister and broken her neck. Philip took it hard, Bill and I returned home with him. When we arrived; Mr. Andrews was in the garage. He had committed suicide.

"It was horrible, Jobi was sitting on the floor holding their father's body. She was like stone. No one has ever been able to get her to remember what happened.

"His mother's body was still in the hallway. Bill found her when he went to call for help. Jobi would not move, it was like she was frozen. We had no idea how long she'd been on that floor. Her nightgown was soaked with his blood. After the funeral, she went to live with her mother's brother in Allerton County so Philip could finish school, but his heart was not in it.

"Jobi was causing all kinds of problems. She would hitchhike over here and break into the house looking for her father. Philip came home after the first semester and re-opened his father's insurance agency. They both lived in the family home until she married Bill."

Marcy cuts the car to the shoulder and kills the engine. Her eyes sparkle with unshed tears. She reaches out to me. "How terrible. I was so angry with him for mistreating his horse. He could have killed himself.

"I didn't know; so much has happened. I shouldn't have made fun of Jobi. It's no wonder she's half crazy. When we were young she was always different. Bill is all she has. . . ."

Her tears spill but she makes no effort to wipe them away. I want to take her in my arms, hold her to chase the demons but her reserve is a wall I can never penetrate. I hand her my handkerchief and light another cigarette.

She blots her face, blows her nose. and takes my cigarette. "Do you realize what a director in Hollywood would give for an actor with a face like Philip's? He doesn't have a bad angle. His sad blue eyes and sun-streaked brown hair would make any woman weep before she collapsed at his feet. Combine his devastating looks with a shadowed past, and every agent in town would be fighting to sign him.

"I don't know what I'm talking about. He doesn't need the fame lane to destroy him, he's succeeding, all on his own. A lifetime. None of our lives have been what we expected the night we graduated."

"No. I never know when I meet Philip on the street if he will be my high school friend or a complete stranger. He rides as if devils are chasing him. John Henry usually exercises one of his mares when he comes out to ride, to keep him from foundering a fine animal. The bay stallion belongs to Philip. He must have arrived after we left the stables. I am sorry you had to see it."

"I'm sorry too. It hurts when you know there is nothing you can do to help an old friend. We can't remake our past."

She starts the car and we drive back to town in complete silence, each adrift in thoughts of a friend we have lost.

CHAPTER 7

The screen door slams. I push papers aside and get to my feet.

"Sit down, Elton, it's just me."

"I know." No one slams a door like Marcy. Even the sound radiates energy. I wait for her to pull a chair up to my desk.

"Can you go with me to look at a house? It's a little one out near the old Hutchins' place. It needs some work, but at the Wren, I can't go to the bathroom in peace."

"I would love to go, but Kathryn Burton has asked me to represent Mese Burrows in her court this morning."

"Court? You all didn't say anything about Kathryn being a judge yesterday."

"Victor Davis had her appointed to fill out Sam Reynolds term, when he died."

"In Brewster County? How did that happen? She's English, isn't she?"

"Her mother was. Irish, actually. She grew up in Ireland during the war. Her father is a general, a bluff character from the old school. He claims John Henry said the magic word—horses—and she told him to marry her the first time she saw him. Her uncle is the Earl of Bathenshire. He sent me the bowl on the mantle."

"Victor Davis? Wasn't he called Good-for-Nothing Davis?"

I find myself laughing at her memory. "Same man."

"Aunt Cynthia referred to him as a social climber. Did he think appointing Kathryn a judge would get him invited to their Derby parties?"

"If he did, it did not work. I go out for a few minutes but I have never seen him at the farm. Their guests are the owners who breed their mares to John Henry's stallions and buyers who want a preview of the new foals.

"He was upset in the last election. A new man from Buckston, Gilbert Harrington, sneaked in on his blind-side."

"Elton, you are a dear. You're kin to John Henry. The derby party at River Cliff Farms is the premier social event in Brewster County." She tilts her head to the left and smiles.

"I'm not making you late with my chatter? I'd love to see Kathryn as a judge; she is an exquisite lady of the manor. May I go with you?"

"It is a simple civil custody hearing. Are you sure you will not be bored?"

She takes the green scarf from her neck and pulls it around her hair like a babushka, but Marcy doesn't look like a grandmother. Her blue-denim skirt with a chunky gold belt looping her hips may be too short for our courtroom but she looks marvelous to me.

"It will be a new experience. I've never been in a courtroom."

* * * * *

I feel a breath of awe tighten my chest each time I enter our old walnut-paneled courtroom with paintings of whiskered judges who have presided in it's environs. Kathryn's portrait, though solemn, lends a hint of compassion to the austere gallery. Today, I am especially proud to have Marci Layne on my arm.

Joan Butcher's high, shrill voice rings across the stillness in righteous indignation, "I spoke to her when she first got here. She didn't even recognize me. When I think of all the things I did for her when we were in high school."

I cannot protect her. I had forgotten who might be present for this hearing in my delight to have her company. Members of the Ladies Auxillary attend court sessions. I cover her hand with mine and look down, silently asking if she wants to leave. She shakes her head and looks straight in front of her.

Nancy Sharp contributes a cutting evaluation. "All she was ever interested in were the boys; she was never one of us. Bill Leighton couldn't breathe unless she was there standing next to him, rubbing against him." The silence is deafening as others notice our presence, but the Ladies Auxiliary are deep in conversation.

Eloise Cutter adds more old gossip as I cringe with embarrassment for them. "I heard Cynthia Lane wouldn't receive her. Poor Miss Lane, just because she's rich and famous, she must think we don't remember how she left. Ran off with a drummer; Jobi told me about seeing her get in his car ages ago."

"How dare she think she could come prancing home after her own husband left her." Nancy draws a quick breath almost hissing as we pass their pew. She puts her nose defiantly in the air, daring the others to silence her.

"I read about someone just like her in one of Callie's *True Confession* magazines. You know how movie stars get their start. . .they call it the casting couch."

Marcy's hand tightens on my arm. Her face carved in marble with no expression as she hears every vicious word. The green eyes glitter for an instant then she straightens her spine until she seems taller.

I seat her on the bench behind the defendant's table where she will get the breeze from the open window. Then give her a bow for a grand performance and take my chair next to my client. Mese Burrows looks at me with vague blue eyes of bewilderment. He has lost all knowledge of why he is here.

Elroy Harris and Lon Chamber bring in the children, Talmus and his sister, Sunshine. What are those two doing here? I assume they would stay clear of courts. They take seats behind Marcy but Sunny refuses to sit with them and rushes to climb in Mese's lap.

Ephriam Flanders is taking a seat behind the plaintiff's table, his face clearly showing his contempt for a hearing he considers a waste of his time and patience. He is joined by Dan Sommers.

Victor Davis peeks through the crack in the doors to make his the last entrance. He escorts Simon Haskins, minister of The Apostle Holiness Church, and his wife Odessa to their chairs in grand style, ignoring the fact that a civil hearing requires no jury for him to impress. When Gilbert Harrington assumes office in January; his name will be inscribed on the pages of dubious achievement.

We rise for Judge Burton's entrance. Victor Davis brushes his hair back from his face and ponderously rises to his feet. He begins addressing Judge Burton before she has a chance to sit. He is holding a slim folder.

"Your Honor, this is a simple matter of jurisdiction and can be settled for the county in my office." He shakes a thick finger toward her as if chastising the court for pursuing an insignificant case.

"Reverend Haskins brought to my attention the plight of two burned children currently residing at the home of Mese Burrows. Mr. Burrows is unable to give proper care to the children financially, nor can his age or mentally capacity, contribute to their welfare. The children are transients with no claim to the resources of Brewster County."

Davis's words are slow and indulgent, as if the defendant and his counsel are disregarding the importance of the county attorney's time to bring the case into open court. The county fund for indigent children is under Davis's jurisdiction, to protect the public from unscrupulous claims. I found no record of Mese's requesting financial aid for the children. Maud Tosh helped me early this morning. It is doubtful Mese knows such aid exists.

Kathryn's voice is strained, "Thank you, for your opening statement Mr. Davis. The court wishes to hear all sides of the matter before rendering a decision. Please call your first witness."

Dan Sommers, though new to the office of sheriff and nervous, describes for the court the circumstances of the children. Their mother had been camping out in one of the abandoned cottages that had been built on the old Hutchins' place before the lake was impounded. A Coleman camp stove exploded.

When the fire-truck arrived, the children had both been burned. The little girl had apparently been lying on a pallet close to the stove. The mother died of smoke inhalation and no identity has been forthcoming. The whereabouts of the father are unknown. The young boy, who is about seven told Dan his sister's name was Sunshine and his was Talmus, but he was unable to supply a surname.

Doc Flanders explains to Kathryn his involvement in the case. The two badly burned children were brought to the hospital last winter after the fire that killed their mother. Mese Burrows, a kindly old man who works as an orderly, cared for them and then took them home with him. Their mother was dead and the county did not have the kind of facilities necessary to provide the intense care Mese had been giving them at the hospital.

Anger clouds his voice as he testifies to the fact that the children are receiving excellent care. Talmus is registered for school using the last name of Burrows, and their burns are healing satisfactorily. His disdain for the blatant bigotry disguised as public concern is palpable, though he is not pointing at the Haskins or Davis.

The ugly truth is there are two Negro children living in the home of a simple white man. The Haskinses perch on the edge of their chairs as if they are ready to take flight in the wake of Doc's wrath. Davis makes a valiant effort to present his clients' concerns but his rhetoric is not enough to defend the indefensible. He is building up to denouncing how Mese Burrows' income is insufficient to cover expenses and the children will be better provided for in a state institution when Elroy leaps to his feet.

"Your Honor, Sir. . .Ma'am. I request permission to speak to the court."

Kathryn removes her hand from her robe where I suspect she has hidden it to prevent the court from seeing her clinched fist. It is obvious why she called last night and asked me to defend Mese.

"Mr. Harris, does your request pertain to the proceeding before the court?"

"Yes, Ma'am."

"This man is interrupting my summation. I object, Your Honor."

"Your objection is noted, Mr. Davis. Mr. Harris, please inform the court why you are here."

"Your Honor. Mr. Harris is a felon—a well-known bootlegger. I object in the name of the plaintiffs."

"Sheriff Sommers, has Mr. Harris or Mr. Chambers ever been arrested?"

"I've tried, Ma'am, but I've never been able to catch 'em."

"Mr. Harris, have you ever been arrested?"

"No, Your Honor, Sir. . .Ma'am."

"I get your point, continue."

"Sorry, Ma'am. I've never seen a court with a lady judge."

Kathryn is holding her breath to suppress a smile. "You are familiar with legal proceedings?"

"Yes, Ma'am. These youngens haven't been a burden to the county, as Davis would have you believe."

"Mr. Harris, are you aware of the grave expense of a burn injury?"

The fans fly but the spectators lean forward in their seats. Mrs. Haskins hides her eyes with her hands but her fingers are spread as Elroy peels off his shirt. "Yes, Ma'am, and I wasn't a growin'."

I hear Marcy's low gasp and moan. Mese hides Sunshine's head in his shoulder.

The puckered ropes of scars around his neck and down his back and chest are horrible. I want to turn my head from the atrocious sight. How can a human being endure what he must have suffered? I vow I will never complain of pain again.

"I see. Thank you for the demonstration. You may put on your shirt."

"Ma'am, when you're growin' the scars must be cut to allow the body to expand. If it isn't done, your bones are encased in a straight jacket of your own skin.

"Mr. Chambers and I took Sunny to Cincinnati to the Schriner's burn hospital. The doctors took time to explain her treatment and how to ease the itching so she won't scratch in her sleep and cause an infection. We have to take her back every six months until she's full grown. Them Schriners won't let a child suffer no matter what the color of their skin."

Elroy turns and shoots the Haskinses a look from green eyes the same shade as Marcy's that nails them to their seats. I want to cheer his courage in stating the real issue.

"The court was not aware of the magnitude of the treatment."

"This case is simple like Mr. Davis said. You tell Elton to draw up legal papers for Mese to have custody or adopt. We'll take care of the rest."

"Mr. Harris, you and Mr. Chambers have no visible means of support. The court. . . ."

He whirls around to face me.

"Elton, what does she mean? We pay our bills."

"Mr. Harris, she means, if I do the paperwork for Mr. Burrows you will have to get a day job."

"Oh!"

Marcy hands me a note, which I take time to read. Sunshine is gripping a lock of her hair over Mese's shoulder.

Let them do it. They are good for children.

I will help with finances.

For a brief instant the courtroom dissolves. I can smell fresh manure; I remember the tall man whose dark skin glistened on the sharp planes of his face as he held the reins of a Welsh pony. My father walking away, leaving me to learn I was not different when riding a horse.

Talmus and Sunshine are in the finest hands with Mese as their custodian and Lon and Elroy as their guardians. I rise from my seat.

"Your Honor, we will handle the matter without any drain on the county's resources. I request these proceedings be adjourned if you have no further instructions."

"Mr. Davis, do not object. I will not tolerate it. I do have one request before I close this session of the court.

"Mr. Harris, will you show Mr. Burrows how to launder their clothes? He is using too much starch."

"Yes, Sir! Your Honor. . .Ma'am."

CHAPTER 8

As we start down the steps of the courthouse, every member on the magistrate's bench is barging their way out of the pool hall as black smoke pours out the side window. Harry Bidwell, Vernon Mayhew, Kyle Thornton, Saxon Pierce and Blake Sanders all blend into the gathering crowd. They strive to appear as nothing more than innocent bystanders while holding their cue sticks. It is obvious the gentlemen were having a secret meeting, as Hiram Mayhew, the clerk-recorder is the last to exit the building.

Above our heads, the siren blows. Marcy clasps her hands over her ears, and I follow suit. The sound blasts in our eardrums, numbing our senses.

"Damn fools. Get out of my way," yells Vern Osborne. "Someone, turn that damn thing off." He pushes us aside and races across the park.

He fights his way through the gawkers and into his building. Around the square, doors and windows fly open as people strain to discover the cause of the commotion.

Mercifully, the shrill whistle stops, though our heads pulse with the vibrations. Every dog in town is howling, their owners screaming to quiet the dim.

Elroy pushes Sunny into Marcy's arms, trailing after Vern. Lon pauses long enough to place Tal's hand in mine before he follows suit and disappears into the building.

We wait suspended on the steps. Tal squeezes my hand, "Mr. Elroy's been burned. He can't burn again, can he?" His large eyes and face are pinched with fear.

"No, son. He'll come be out in a minute." I pray I am not lying to him. Time is counted by the grip of the small hand in mine before Lon reappears with the grease trap to the grill blazing on the blade of a shovel. He dumps it upside down at the edge of the road by the square and starts to dig, throwing shovel after shovel of dirt over the smoking box.

Tal's small hands are clapping with glee behind the back of our mayor. Simon Blake has positioned himself for the clearest view, and is now ignoring the small child straining to see around him.

Elroy and Vern come out the door carrying a large case. I start laughing, an inappropriate response. They have risked their lives to save the simulated horse racing machine. Not one thought have they given to the contents of the Masonic Lodge hall above the poolroom. They carry it across the square to the corner.

"Elton, that's the infamous horse-track. They're taking it to your office."

"Bring the children." I start after Vern and Elroy as the fire engine turns the corner into the square. Rupert Tosh is at the wheel.

"Take it back to the barn, Rup. We got it under control." Vern yells.

For what seems like the first time since we opened the courthouse door, I take a deep breath of relief. Our equipment is limited at best and a major fire would be a disaster.

"This is where you've been." Louise Bidwell stalks from the jewelry store with long strides. She takes Harry's arm and walks him back across the square. "I've been looking for you all morning."

Marcy giggles beside me. "Except for the crowd of on-lookers she'd have taken him by the ear," as we hurry to my office.

"Now Elton, it's only until repairs are made to the premises."

"Vern, that is an illegal betting machine."

"No, it isn't. It's a historical artifact. I bought it at the auction of a gas station in Dixon. This track is famous, never throws a race."

The odor of burning grease follows Lon through the front door. "Fire's out; everyone is going home. I opened all the windows to air out the smoke. Mese has the children in the park on the swings."

"Elroy, this is my law office. It is not appropriate to house that here. I have to think of my clients."

"You're the best in town. You learned to bet on that machine like every other kid in the county. Why do you think we brought it here instead of taking it to the bank?"

"We girls only heard rumors. You have no idea, the sins we imagined. Secret vices of the male species exposed. This is wonderful. Where is Tom Clement? I have an expose of the century."

"Marcy gal, have your fun. We are leaving the track with Elton for safe-keeping. No yahoo will try to rig it."

"Elton doesn't mind; he just likes to fuss. I'll come

back tonight and he can teach me to play. But where are we going to get a decent hamburger?"

"You have gone in the pool hall?"

"In that exclusive all-male club. No way. I send the guy at the desk of the Wren. He brings it up to my room with a sack of potato chips and a Coke. It's what passes for room service at the Wren."

* * * * *

"Marcy, this is the Farmington homeplace. The Corps moved the house up here above the high water. It is not fit for chickens to use as a roost."

"Yes, it is. Look, these floors are chestnut with hedge-apple joists, I've been down in the cellar. Aunt Cynthia says they're the best, bugs can't live in them."

"It does not have a lake view. There is not a neighbor for two miles in either direction. Why?"

"It's perfect; no one else wants it. Elton, you haven't lived where every move you make is reported in a newspaper. I want privacy and peace."

"Will you let me have Adam Young come out to check the structure? If he says it is sound, then let him renovate it for you."

"Fine by me. Adam Young? Do I know him?"

"He was several years behind us in school but quit to help at home."

"I remember. He has a swarm of little brothers."

"Same person, but the brothers are grown. All are over six foot and have finished or are working on university educations. Except for Jim, the youngest. He quit school to become involved in automobile racing. When he is home, he helps Adam, who is a builder. Adam will do a first class-job."

"Wait a minute, one of them could sing. Isaiah Young, he sang in church. I saw his name in Wednesday's *Banner*; he's singing at the Rock House. Let's go, I haven't been dancing forever."

* * * * *

The Rock House is located at the edge of the Tennessee/Kentucky line. It has not changed in the years since I was in college. It still has the same long bar, with mismatched tables and chairs scattered around a small dance floor. The kitchen may be in Kentucky, but the bar is in Tennessee, where liquor is legal. Neon beer signs adorn the walls. All the windows are open, ceiling fans turning, but the crowded room is thick with the blue haze of cigarette smoke.

The music has improved. Isaiah Young has a clear tenor voice that is well matched by his brother Isaac's baritone. They have a crowd-pleasing style, which I enjoy as I sip a Falls City beer and watch Marcy dance with Philip.

Philip teased her for being incognito. She is wearing ordinary jeans, a plaid shirt tied at the waist, with a Mennonite straw boater. Her hair is covered with a bandanna. Glasses complete the effect: large black-framed squares of plain glass not sunglasses. She has not been recognized; she can enjoy the music.

She intends to keep him sober for dancing; when Philip is not looking she has been pouring part of his beer in the plant behind our table. They make fine dance partners, and I envy him.

"Elton. Slumming tonight?"

"Bill! We came to hear the Youngs."

"I was on my way home from Crossville when I saw

your car." Bill looks toward the dance floor, where Philip and Marcy are twirling to a western swing tune, *Gonna Get Tight.* "Is he okay? He doesn't need that kind of encouragement."

"So far, Marcy has been watering the plant with his beer."

"I wouldn't count on it working. He carries a flask and uses beer as a chaser."

"Is it that bad?"

"I'm afraid so. I think he's trying to kill himself." Bill is concerned for Philip but his eyes follow Marcy with the hunger of a starving man.

As if reading my thoughts, he takes a chair. "You'd best order some hamburgers and fries. The grease will help because if I know Philip he hasn't eaten all day. He weighs less than one-fifty from consuming liquid meals." He runs nervous fingers through his thick brown hair, a gesture I have never seen him use.

Adam Young and his wife Vera pause by our table. They are wearing identical white turtleneck sweaters and dark slacks. A very handsome couple.

"Mr. Fightmaster, I went by the house as you asked. Doesn't look like much but, structurally, it's sound. Give it a coat of paint, new shingles on the roof, caulk around the windows, and rehang the doors. Nothing major, just cosmetic work. Kitchen and bath can stand replacing but it depends on how much you want to put into it."

"Thank you, Adam. When can you start the work?"

He points to the stage, "The twins are working for their spending money. Isaiah got a teaching fellowship for his master's. Isaac was accepted to law school at Northwestern. I could send them out on Monday."

Marcy and Philip are making their way back when Vera spots her.

"That's Marci Layne!" She squeals in my ear but is drowned out by the band and conversation in the room. How can Isaiah stand the terrible acoustics with his university-trained ear?

"The work is for Miss Layne. I'll call the lumber yard to set up an account for whatever you need, but she will tell you what she wants."

I make the introductions. Vera demands an autograph, which Marcy scribbles on a bar napkin before dragging Adam to a far corner while Philip, ever the gallant, escorts Vera to the dance floor.

Bill goes to the bar to order food for us. I do not care for roadhouse cooking, but if it will keep Philip sober through the evening, I will endure it. The new chef at the country club has a light hand, even with vegetables.

The twins start a tune I remember hearing on the radio before I started high school, *What It Means to Be Blue*. It suits my mood. I lean back to listen while Bill sips his beer, his eyes fixed on Marcy. I sense disaster looming on the horizon.

Adam and Marcy shake hands on their deal and he reclaims his wife from Philip. They join us as the burgers arrive, which are surprisingly excellent. Even Philip starts eating with enthusiasm. I hear the heavy bass beat of another oldie, *I'm Talkin' About You*. Where did the boys find these songs? They are not using sheet music. The twins are so different. Isaac is over six foot but Isaiah is even taller, with rather sad amber eyes to his brother's dark brown.

I am sure the entire room is buzzing about our table but we are allowed to eat in peace without demands for autographs.

Isaac announces they are going to do a medley of Eddie Arnold standards. The opening strains of *The Last Word in*

Lonesome is Me fill the room. Bill holds his hand out to Marcy. They do not say a word as he follows her to the dance floor. I want to bring her back to the table and start to get up, but Philip pulls me down before I make a fool of myself.

"It had to happen. You can't prevent the inevitable, and it's a public dance floor."

My heart withers as I watch their bodies meld as if they never lived separate lives. Isaiah croons, *Make the World Go Away* as Bill's hand caresses her back.

Philip is right; I hate to admit it but it was always Marcy and Bill. We were planets, spinning around their sun. The entire world now stands between them, but for a few minutes they escape into themselves, held this side of respectable by her hat. Philip and I are useless chaperons as the boys finish with *I'll Hold You in My Heart*.

Philip grips his head in his hands, "I don't want to watch; my sister will kill her—or him—or both." He drops his head on the table, it rests on his folded arm. I want to join him; I hurt for them.

They walk back to the table, side-by-side but not touching. "I'll take him home with me. It will explain why I'm so late. Philip. . . ." He shakes him and Philip raises his head. "Come on, you're going with me."

"Best idea I've heard all night." His words are slurred as he staggers to his feet, leaning on the table.

Marcy sits beside me and we watch Bill help Philip to the door. She picks up Philip's drink and takes a sip. "My God, this is vodka disguised as beer."

"Bill said he cheated."

"Elton, waltz with me and don't say a word."

The one dance I can manage is a waltz. We finish

the evening with *The Tennessee Waltz*. Isaiah and Isaac sing it twice for us, then we follow our friends into the night.

I have lost the girl I never had, to a guy she can never have, and we both know it.

CHAPTER 9

A small dark hand appears from behind Marcy's back. It carefully places a glass of ice water above her knife, then disappears. Talmus Burrows comes to my side of the table and repeats the motion, his face stern with concentration. The child is a picture: a short chef's helper's white hat almost covers his eyes, held fast in the back with a diaper pin. A large apron is tied around his neck. The long strings crisscross over his chest and circle his middle where the heavy cloth is folded double to prevent it from dragging the floor.

"Thank you, Tal." My voice startles him; he looks up with frightened eyes. "Very nice." His face beams at the compliment.

A bright grin reveals one big front tooth and a gap. He is younger than Sheriff Sommers estimated. "Mr. Wilson says I must save my tips for college. I'm going to school next week."

"Who is Mr. Wilson?"

Tal waves a thin arm toward the kitchen. "He cooks, sir. I'm his. . .gopher."

I do not dare look at Marcy. I know her eyes are dancing with laughter for the serious child.

"Loaning Elroy your car to take Sunshine to the clinic was nice. Mine doesn't have enough seats."

The flat nasal voice of a native New Yorker comes from the lips of the strangest looking man I have ever seen. He is young, but looks old. His shirt is a bright yellow with wide pink stripes, his trousers are lavender. . .lavender. The outrageous clothes are covered with an apron like Tal's but a tall head-chef's hat rests on tight-brown curls over his ears.

"New York, I think the Bronx."

"Yes, sir, how did you know?"

"Your voice. I had a classmate in law school who sounded like you."

His darting brown eyes twinkle for just a moment. "Tal is staying with me until they get back. He insisted on helping, and it keeps him busy. Children get bored when they have nothing to do. Is every thing to your taste, Miss Layne?"

Marcy pats her stomach in a beguiling gesture. "I'm stuffed, even if I can't get near anyone except Elton for the rest of the afternoon. He smells, too. Freedom is eating real garlic. Your scampi was fantastic."

She extends her hand to Mr. Wilson. "Marcy Lane; Elton forgot to introduce me." She gives it the local pronunciation, not the French sound of her screen name.

He takes it reverently, shaking her hand. "Robert Curtis Wilson. Elroy said you were a gracious lady. Thank you for enjoying my food. We have fresh ambrosia for desert."

"Perfect."

* * * * *

"Do I drop you off at home?"

"Yes, it feels strange to be on foot, though days go by when I do not move my car. Its presence is reassuring. The new chef is impressive."

"Elton, don't be such a stuffed-shirt. If you had dentures you would've dropped them when you saw him. Admit it."

"He does look strange."

"Elton, he's gay."

"I would assume he is happy."

"I doubt it. More than likely, he's miserable at times. What I meant was he is a homosexual."

"Oh, dear. Why would he come to Brewster County?"

"I have no idea, it's not the liberal capital of the world. Funny, though, he has a Marine tattoo on his arm. I'm sure that is what I saw when he reached for my hand."

"It did not bother you to shake hands with him?"

"Why should it? Elton, many people in Hollywood are homosexuals, both men and women, many of them are very talented and creative. The guy who does my makeup for my films is gay. Jean Harlow was married to a homosexual and it's rumored Angela Lansbury's first husband was gay.

"Some well-known actors have all kinds of stories circulating about them that are very carefully kept out of the papers by their studios.

"I'll tell you one thing, in time of trouble they don't let you down if they consider you a friend. I know. Give Mr. Robert Curtis Wilson a chance.

"Don't look surprised; I caught that middle name. He might be a cousin. He seems like a nice kid, but very nervous; he never actually looked at us, not once."

CHAPTER 10

Clayton Forrester came by last week; he found his place in Allerton County. I made up the deed for him to record and he has returned to California. He plans to build a cabin next spring; I look forward to getting to know him again. Too many of my friends have left Brewster County for greener pastures. I know Marcy will leave too; her career is in California.

I am wearing a sweater. Winter is around the corner, and the leaves have scattered across my lawn like a tapestry. It is so quiet even the birds and insects are taking a nap. I have not seen Marcy until almost dark for over two weeks. I cannot remember the days being so long until she came home. She is supervising the remodeling of her house and she stops to bring the Young twins back to town before supper.

We eat together most evenings, sometimes at the Wren or, if she is feeling festive we go out to the country club for one of Robert Wilson's magnificent dinners. It is tempting to sneak in a young Beaujolais to have with his *roti de boeuf aux champignons et marrons* but so far we have settled for sweet tea and a French lesson. Roast beef with mushrooms and chestnuts is delicious in any language. He says Les Rugiens Pommard is a great burgundy, and he will bring some back if he goes to New York.

I look up from my paper as wheels crunch on the gravel of my driveway. James Bond's *Goldfinger* car is pulling in behind my Buick. Robert Wilson gets out and gently pats the hood before he crosses to the porch.

"My pride and joy, won her in a crap game just before I mustered out of the service. She's been a good luck charm ever since. Good, you're reading the paper. Please turn to the back page."

For him, his costume (I refuse to call them clothes) is very subdued: a navy shirt with chartreuse slacks. They would be less glaring if he would reverse his color scheme. He has an old book with papers sticking out from the pages tucked under his arm.

I fold the paper and turn it over. As usual Real Estate ads cover the back page. "Yes?"

"Down near the bottom, the one about settling the estate of a Cal Osborne."

"I see it. He died last year."

"I'm interested in buying the diner."

"The diner. You mean the one out on the state highway going south?"

"Yes. Elroy will bid for me so a local won't run up the price. Will you do the paperwork? He said you were the only honest lawyer in Clydsville. I can pay with a check or get cash." He stands on the top step looking expectant and talking fast while clutching the book.

"That diner has been closed since I was in high school. Mr. Osborne left one day and never came back." I get to my feet. "Come in and we will talk about it."

"Pretty lady." He points. "Tough old bird."

I cannot help laughing, he has described my parents with five words. "Sit down, Robert."

"Call me Wilson. Everybody does. Look, don't climb my hide. Elroy and Lon have already worked it over, but I want my own place. I know it isn't much, a half-a-mile out of town, but it has potential. There is an apartment upstairs. . . . "

"There is? I do not remember anyone ever living there."

"Elroy says soldiers bunked up there during the war."

"That was before my time."

"A bus stopped out front to pick them up and took them to camp. Some guys lived there while they were working on the dam."

"Now, that makes sense. We never have had much in the way of accommodations for visitors. I remember a tent city out by the dam site. Can it be repaired so you will not be wasting your money?"

"Lon and Elroy are willing to help. It has land around it so when the town grows I won't be crowded. There's plenty of space for a garden and a television antenna-tower."

He seems so sure Clydsville is going to grow; to me it seems we are losing people every year. Elroy Harris and Lon Chambers avoid strangers, but this man is using their name frequently.

"You spend time with them?"

He opens the book and hands me some worn papers. "My oldest brother was in their unit in North Africa. They were with him when he died. These are his letters. There is a letter Lon Chambers wrote Mother. She always maintained it was the most beautiful letter a mother ever received about her fallen son.

"She didn't know he was colored until they visited on their way home after the war. I was about two or three at the time and don't remember, but they took dinner with the family at the restaurant. In a sense Elroy and Lon replaced John in my mother's eyes and became members of our family. They kept in touch with Christmas cards and a rare letter from Lon.

"While they were talking at the restaurant, my father realized his parents were originally from Brewster County, though his father died in West Virginia in a mining accident when he was small. Both my grandmother and father cooked for the DeMarcos, then Dad bought them out when he married their daughter. They kept the name, which helped it to survive the Depression. A neighborhood family restaurant, people knew they could get a good meal for a fair price.

"Wait a minute. DeMarco's, the Italian restaurant in New York?"

"Yes, half belongs to my brother Constantine, and my sister Frederica and I inherited our mother's half. So you see, cooking is in my blood. It's the only thing I know how to do.

"Frederica has been keeping my things until I get settled. Their apartment is small."

"Wilson is not an Italian name." I watch this strange young man staring at the floor and moving the book from hand to hand as he tells his story.

"I'm the youngest son of a West Virginia coal miner's son and an Italian immigrant's daughter. My mother was Annetta DeMarco."

I hold the thin dry letters that have been read so often the folds are splitting and the ink fading. A mother's connection to a lost son, they are not mine to read. I hand them back to Wilson.

"Before my mother died, she insisted I take them with my grandmother's diary and come to Brewster County. Constantine doesn't want an abomination like me in New York. He doesn't have much use for Frederica, either, because she married Bernard Stein, a Jew. We both ignore him. He banished me, almost like my grandparents were banished from Brewster County. So I don't have much of a family, except Elroy and Lon, who knew my brother who died the year before I was born."

He sits slumped in loneliness, holding the worn book between his hands, a fragile link to his family.

Suddenly I remember my father's bedroom, where the Curtis' family Bible rests on the stand by the window. My grandmother's, most prized possession, which I was never allowed to touch, with a violent ink slash through a name.

"Wilson, will you wait? It will take me a few minutes."

"Yes, sir."

I climb the stairs as fast as I can, because a mystery of my childhood is near a solution. I would steal into my father's room to finger the forbidden book. It was old when it became his property.

I take my great-grandfather's Bible from the stand and go back downstairs to retreat behind my desk not knowing how I feel about Wilson's nature. My prejudices are irrelevant; he deserves to learn the truth. The book opens to the page of its own volition.

"Wilson, the book you are holding is your grandmother's diary?"

"Yes." His voice is almost a whisper.

"You have the middle name of Curtis. I assume it was

your grandmother's maiden name."

He looks up at me, straight at me for the first time. "Come around my desk, I have something you need to see. The Curtis family Bible."

He fingers the page, tracing the dark line as I did in childhood.

"My grandmother's name: Emma Louise Curtis, has been marked out."

I sense the anger in his stance as if he wants to crumble the page in his fist.

"Wilson, my grandmother was her sister, Martha Burton Curtis. You are my second cousin. Who did she marry that angered her father so much?"

"John Laurence Wilson."

"How is Laurence spelled?" He tells me it has a "u" instead of the normal "w" and I start laughing. He looks at me, stunned.

"Welcome to a rather large family, Wilson. You are related to most of the people you have met in Brewster County.

"Our great-grandfathers were very early robber-barons of fame and fable. Fierce rivals who savaged the hills for virgin timber, shipping it to Nashville by river.

"The houseboats Elroy and Lon live on may have been built from logs they cut. Later it was coal and anything else where a dollar could be made. They fought each other tooth and nail and with a few bullets. Your grandmother married a member of the hated rival family with a middle name of Laurence. I am not sure where the name Wilson enters your history."

He goes back to a chair and drops down. "She doesn't mention what happened, in her diary. Are you sure, Sir?"

"Positive and stop calling me sir. Elton will be fine. It will take some getting with a few family members to piece the story together. Something we can do this winter, for now you want to purchase a piece of property."

CHAPTER 11

The shrill of the courthouse siren assaults my ears like a lost memory from weeks past. I have been dreaming and start to turn over but the blast is relentless.

Morning is early. I feel as though I just went to bed. My room is aglow with bright light streaming in the windows. The ringing continues as I turn over to stare at the clock, one a.m!

Fire! Something is on fire on the square. My dressing is never swift but I hurry, grabbing a robe nearest to hand, not bothering with the brace. I make it down the stairs without falling, clutch the old crutches and hobble to the corner.

The Wren. Marcy is in the hotel! Panic speeds my feet as I probe through the crowd collected on the square just as flames burst through the roof. Screams I dare not utter choke my throat. Terror propels me forward.

A hand grabs my arm. "No, Elton, stop." Philip Andrews is pulling me back from the holocaust.

"Marcy? Where is she?" I stare at the burning wood structure as the roof collapses into the pile. No one caught in their beds could be alive in this inferno.

"She wasn't in her room. We couldn't find her. We broke down every door upstairs." I try to pull away but his grip cuts to the bone. "Elton, listen to me, she wasn't in the hotel." He is yelling in my ear as if I am deaf. I begin to tremble. Where is she?

"We had time to get everybody out. Harry Bidwell helped." Philip is holding my arm and shaking me. It started in that extra room Marcy rented at the back. That's what gave us time to evacuate the permanent borders. Their rooms were on the ground floor."

He shoves me onto a bench as my leg gives. "Don't even think it. You can't go in there. The hotel is gone." His face is streaked with black grime, but he is stone-cold sober.

Greasy fumes billow in the heavy smoke. It is hard to breathe. The roar of a tremendous explosion sends yellow pyramids shooting high into the night sky from the back of the structure.

For a moment all I can see is a blur of black smoke with a fierce blue surrounded by red and yellow flames. I cannot stop the tears that flow down my face. I am so helpless, unable to save her from danger as I had so often dreamed. I watch Philip rush over to the tight knot of bewildered hotel residents. He is definitely sober, able to help while all I can do is sit on a park bench. As useless as my father proclaimed me to be.

Tom Clement sinks down beside me, his face smeared with sweat and soot. He reaches out, "Get a grip Elton. She wasn't in the hotel nor is her car in the parking lot. I will not have to print the lurid headlines, 'Marci Layne Dies in Hotel Fire.' Her rooms were empty. I got a quick glimpse in the one she used as a bedroom. The bed was made."

Relief takes more out of me than pain. I lean back against the bench and begin to breathe the acrid fumes. "Her car is not behind the hotel?"

"I just told you, it's not in town."

"Where is she?"

"Elton, she is a grown woman who does not have to check in with you when she goes out. Now calm down. She'll show. We checked the register to make sure everyone is accounted for before the building collapsed. Harry Bidwell rescued it from off the desk. She has not checked out."

He makes me feel like an old woman peeking at the neighbors. Could she have agreed to meet Bill on this of all nights? The house. In my panic I have forgotten the house and her deep desire for privacy. She might have gone out there. The magazines said that she took long drives in California at night after her daughter was lost; reporters had followed her.

Three elderly women have lost their homes, friends of my mother, and I have not had a thought for them. I pray Marcy is safe.

I watch Tom go toward the smoldering ruins of the hotel. Sharp bangs crack like exploding fire crackers. He runs down the small alley as more small explosions burst from the flames. Dan Sommers races after him. I strain to see what is happening.

I can hear Louise Bidwell's clear voice from the other side of the square. "Since Gloria married Stanton Sidmore, Mama has been alone. There is plenty of room. Come with me and we'll get things straightened out after everyone has had some rest." She is talking to the huddled hotel residents. Friends and neighbors are pitching in to help. Mrs. Carstairs will love to have the company even if it is under such tragic circumstances.

Everyone is like me, clad in pajamas and robes with top coats hastily pulled over them to keep out the sharp night wind. Survivors of the dreaded bane of our community: fire.

The fear of it breaking out with so many wood structures around the square is a chronic nightmare. Our lone pumper truck is parked over the spring, and Rupert Tosh is manning the pumps. Hoses are strung across the park to the front of the other buildings as men work to contain the inferno. They are soaking roofs to keep the falling sparks from spreading havoc as the flames fold inward on themselves.

My family home stands safe and secure with its slate roof and brick construction. I can see it shadowed against the faint light from the papermill yard. The bank and courthouse are also brick, while the jail is river stone, impervious to any desperate attempt at a jail break, should we ever have a criminal of such magnitude.

One of the reasons I agreed to Marcy's purchasing the little house was its brick facade and metal roof. Much better for out in the county where they don't have a fire truck. I suspect, my agreement had little to do with her decision. I know she can walk to the back of the property and look down on the lake covering the Lane farm where she grew up.

Cynthia Lane and her uncompromising standards of family. Refusing to allow Marcy in the house because she planned to divorce her husband before he was killed. Believing Jobi Leighton's old story of Marcy leaving with a traveling salesman. Marcy is not stupid; she was valedictorian of our class. She must have saved every penny she ever earned to buy a bus ticket to California.

Someone hands me a cup of coffee in a paper cup. I hate drinking from paper cups; it is like being in the hospital all over again. I take a sip, it is good, with the faint taste of hazelnut. Hazelnut?

I look around the square. Wilson's silver Aston Martin is parked on the grass with the trunk open. He is ladling coffee from a large pot while Maud Tosh hands out sandwiches from a small table. Lon lifts the large pot from the trunk, putting it beside Maud's sandwiches. He shuts the lid and Wilson drives away.

"Jobi, you sit here, while I look for Bill." He takes off his jacket and drapes it around her shoulders. Elton, keep an eye on her."

Tom Clement sits Jobi Leighton down beside me. She reeks of gasoline clouded with the heavy odor of Emeraude to liberally applied. She is wearing an evening gown—an evening gown out here at a fire. I take a closer look, her face is smeared with thick makeup, streaked with dirt. Her hair is twisted around those pink rods women use to give each other home permanents.

What's wrong with her? She does not know me. The fixed stare of her eyes is directed toward the fire as if she can see through it.

Tom is almost running. "No sign of Bill, but his car is parked on the far side of the bank. Jobi, where's Bill?"

She does not turn her head at his question. "I'm my Daddy's little love. Bill's gone."

"What? Her daddy has been dead for years. Is she in shock?"

"I believe so. Watch."

I move my hand in front of her eyes; she does not blink.

"I have not seen Bill but Philip is here. I talked to him,

over there by Maud Tosh."

"Keep an eye on her. I found her in the woods behind the hotel. She was sitting on a pile of clothes." Tom takes off, heading for Philip.

Jobi spreads the skirt of the heavy satin gown across the bench. Her thin hands move across the stained fabric, but she gives no indication that she knows where she is. Oh dear, she's like she was the night her parents died, when no one could make her understand, no matter how hard we tried. I replace Tom's jacket on her shoulder. There are socks sticking out of the top of her dress.

Hours pass while Jobi and I sit on the bench waiting for a sign of either Marcy or Bill. Someone takes the empty cup from my limp fingers and gives me a fresh cup of coffee. We wait in the silence of our own thoughts. Like stone she sits; her eyes dead and staring. She does not move when I pull Tom's jacket around her shoulders.

Cadel Beckworth, the president of First Farmers and Gilbert Harrington, the newly-elected county attorney, come strolling across the lawn, drinking coffee and dressed as if they are ready to begin their day. Beckworth nods to Jobi, taking notice of her bizarre appearance.

"Where is Leighton? He shouldn't let his wife wander around drunk. Fightmaster, what happened to the hotel?"

I find it hard to respect this man, much less like him. Jobi either does not hear him or ignores him. She continues to stare at the smoking, smoldering rubble of what was our hotel, now gone with the night.

I struggle to my feet, moving the crutches under my arms for support. Even bent over I can stare down at Beckworth. I answer him with the same tone of pious contempt. "As you can see, Beckworth. The Wren has burned."

Gilbert Harrington looks toward the rubble, "But we

were planning to have breakfast." His bewildered countenance indicates an odd attitude, as if the fire was planned to cause him an inconvenience. His next words prove it.

"Were the hotel people responsible for this disaster?" He is not bright enough to keep the vision of a lucrative lawsuit from flashing across his face.

"Jobi, what have—where's Jobi?" Philip is disheveled, burn-holes pepper his jacket. The air is rent by another series of loud cracks. Roman candle torches burst forth, sending blue and green flames from the smoldering ruins. Beckworth and Harrington jump as if they have been shot.

Dan Sommers, standing behind Philip, smothers his laughter. "Sorry, those are aerosol cans of cleaning stuff exploding, not gunfire. It is too dangerous to find the cause until the state fire marshal arrives to check for other unexploded cans. They instructed me to rope off the entire area for public safety."

"Elton, where did Jobi go?"

"She was here just a moment ago." I look across to Wilson's car, which is pulling in beside Maud's table.

"But I must open the bank. Friday is our busiest day."

"No, not until we get the all-clear. Thanks to the Young boys, you've got a bank to open. They've worked all night to save the roof. Go get some breakfast. I may have a better answer for you this afternoon."

"In case you hadn't noticed, there is nowhere to eat."

Dan's ears turn red beneath his scorched Stetson, but he drills Harrington with an icy stare, noting his clean clothes. "The country club is going to take up the slack. I talked to the new manager."

I see Jobi dragging Tom's coat. She is walking toward the fire, the train of the gown humping over the hoses. I start forward, taking my hand off the bar of the crutch. I begin to topple.

"Philip! Jobi," I point, "catch her, there is gasoline on that dress." I scream at him as a hand closes around my arm, preventing me from falling.

Dan and Philip sprint toward Jobi as Harrington and Beckworth leave the park. Marcy's angry voice hisses behind me, "She's. . .my dress. I wore it to the Academy Awards ceremony."

"Marcy, where were you? I was so worried."

"Making coffee. . . ."

"Mr. Fightmaster, have you seen Jobi or Bill Leighton?"

Dan and Philip have reached Jobi and are bringing her back. The way she was going she would have walked straight into the fire.

Marcy helps me to turn. She is muttering under her breath, but I cannot hear her furious words. Emma Parker is standing behind the crowd waving her arm. She pushes her way through the crowd toward us.

"Little Bill was sitting on their back steps, in nothing but his pajamas, watching the fire. I can't find his parents." Her words are frantic.

Philip has a firm arm around Jobi's shoulders as she fights him.

"Oh! Jobi, you've ruined your pretty dress, it's all stained. You didn't tell me you were going out. I put Little Bill to bed with my kids, that's what you wanted me to do, isn't it?"

Jobi bites Philip's hand and jerks away, but Dan Sommers grabs her as she tries to run back to the hotel. Philip puts his arm around her neck in a choke-hold. "That's fine. . .Mrs. Parker. Jobi isn't feeling well. I'll

come and get him later today. Bill will show up."
Emma's eyes grow as she looks at the strange treatment
of her neighbor.

Dan smiles at her as a blast from the steam whistle
at the papermill erupts, "Ralph is late for work. Go
home, Emma."

Jobi's blank eyes fasten on Marcy, her voice
threaded with viciousness. "I'm my Daddy's little
love. No matter what she said he wouldn't touch you."
Jobi slaps Marcy across the face, knocking her into my
shoulder. I totter on the edge of balance but manage to
keep us both erect.

Stunned, Marcy steps forward, "Why you little. . . ."

"Marcy no, please no." I reach for her. She looks back
at me, holding her cheek where the imprint of Jobi's hand
is turning red. The Lane temper is a near match for the
exploding aerosol cans.

Philip and Dan pull Jobi's hands behind her, both men
holding her. Marcy steps back, beside me, and takes my
arm. Her grip tightens as she fights for control.

Philip looks at me with imploring eyes, "Dan, may I
take her to the hospital? Doc Flanders will have something
to knock her out."

Jobi is struggling in their arms, kicking at Philip's
shins.

"Come on, Philip. I'll drive while you hold her. Watch
her nails, she clawed me." Dan helps him lead Jobi,
stomping and fighting them across the square to where his
cruiser is parked. Marcy picks up, Tom's tweed coat and
pulls it on over her Eisenhower jacket.

The square is silent. The air heavy with smoke, but the
danger has passed. Marcy and I stand alone looking at the
sodden ruins of the Wren. She is safe. My relief is

overwhelming as I look down at her face to see silent tears streaming from her eyes.

"She started the fire." Her abrupt statement confirms my suspicions. "She. . .she. . .destroyed all I had of my daughter."

I have no answer for her, I cannot even wrap my arms around her. She walks beside me as we leave the park, measuring her steps to mine.

CHAPTER 12

Marcy and I enter the Knock Kneed Kricket Kafe, laughing. She has just explained the name to me.

On the peak of the roof sits a large cricket, to get it to stay in place, Elroy and Lon bolted the knees together. Isaiah Young had finished the lettering on the windows yesterday morning just in time for the unexpected opening. The relief of hearing her tinkling-bell sound is marvelous, but she is hiding behind her public face. The stiff tension of her body has not relaxed since we left the park.

She bathed her face with ice to hide to effects of her tears. My lame efforts at comfort offer small conciliation for her loss. She literally has only her purse and the same clothes she wore to the roadhouse. Jobi Leighton had torched the mementos of her luminous career, but even worse was her wanton destruction of the few pictures of the child Marcy grieves for every waking moment.

I did not realize until we fortified ourselves with brandy that Marcy has come home. She left nothing of herself in California. All her important possessions had been in her hotel room waiting to be moved to her new house. She has dropped her screen name spelling.

Marcy has returned to stay, no matter what the cost.

Inside the old diner, major changes are under way. Today, the saw-horses hold rough planks covered with newspaper to serve as a buffet and eating space. The Methodist church has loaned their folding chairs until furniture arrives, but a gleaming kitchen is in place. The old plank floors have been sanded and coated with heavy wax.

Wilson could not possibly have prepared all the food crowding the buffet. As I fill my plate, I recognize contributions from the ladies of Clydsville. The room is packed with friends who worked hard during the night. It is not possible to speak to each one of them. I am proud to be a member of this community, which bands together in the face of adversity.

Tal appears at my side wearing his "gopher" outfit and takes my paper plate to the table. Mese is holding Sunny at the end of the table. Elroy hands me a cup of coffee in a real cup. "When did you start waiting tables?"

"Now, Elton, you told us to get a day job." I know for a fact both he and Lon had fought the fire, soaking the roofs of nearby buildings to give the Youngs a break from holding the heavy hoses upright. They spelled Rupert Tosh on the pumps, then lent a hand wherever one was needed. Wilson waves a knife in greeting as he slices a country ham. Lon is busy working the grill.

Dan Sommers is out of uniform. He looks strange in regular slacks and shirt; a plaid hunting jacket is hanging over the back of his chair. He does not mention the problem with Jobi. He is so tired, Opal is holding his cup. Like the rest of us, he is thinking of going home to catch a few hours sleep.

Tal pulls on his arm. "Sheriff, Mr. Wilson says you're wanted on the telephone. An em. . .emergency."

Dan gets to his feet and follows him to the kitchen where Wilson is holding the phone. He turns his back to the noisy room to listen then slowly returns to the table, looking around.

"Tom, Elton, I don't trust myself to drive. Will you go with me to the country club? Cadel Beckworth and Gilbert Harrington have found Bill Leighton. No, No. Don't ask any questions, I don't know any more. Finish your breakfast, folks."

Maud Tosh looks at Rupert. "Dan, we'll take Opal home. Go do what you have to do." Rupert nods his head in agreement.

"We will take my Buick to pick up your cruiser. I was the last one to arrive. Marcy?"

"Bill may be hurt. Don't worry about me, my car is out back. Hurry."

* * * * *

We stop at the clubhouse, where Beckworth is waiting to give us directions. After they finished breakfast while waiting for the state fire marshal to allow the bank to open, he and Harrington had decided to play a round of golf before returning to town. They found Bill's body on the fifth green by the cup flag.

Tom drives the police cruiser straight across the fairways. Hole five sits on a small hill. It is impossible to see the green until you come up over the edge from the fairway. Tom jerks the cruiser to the left to avoid the sandtrap below the brink of the green.

Gilbert Harrington is sitting above the back edge, his

head in his hands, for once not thinking of his appearance. He rises at the sound of the car, being careful to keep his back to the green.

The green is pristine in the morning sunshine. Two white balls mar its smooth surface. We walk by two putting irons lying crosswise on the edge. Bill is lying near the cup facing the sky.

"It took you long enough. Why the press?" Harrington is furious at being left with the body. He is holding a beer can, which sloshes on his sleeve as he points at Tom.

"I need some help and Tom will have to know for the paper. It's only right."

Harrington is going full-bore, "Fightmaster can't do anything."

"He makes an excellent witness." Dan turns his back and goes to work, ignoring both Harrington and Beckworth, who has not spoken since he told us where they had discovered Bill.

"Are these your footprints?" Dan is pointing to two sets of cleated tracks across the green.

"Of course." Harrington needs to examine his attitude if he wants to succeed as county prosecutor. It is brusk and contemptuous, maybe he resents people from Clydsville? I had hoped that attitude would died when we built a consolidated high school—no more inter-town rivalry.

"Go back to the clubhouse and wait. I'll need to ask you some questions later. Call for the ambulance."

"I know the routine, Sheriff." Oh dear, his defensiveness is unnecessary.

Dan ignores him, his mind clearly on his job. "Tom, use your notebook. Write down every thing I describe."

Bill's face is flushed and puffy, his eyes are open with the same vacant stare Jobi had last night. A thin line of sand trails across the green to the sand pit. The sight of Bill's mangled head as Dan turns him, churns the little breakfast I ate.

Tom gasps in shock, the back of Bill's head has been almost pulverized with repeated blows from a bloody iron lying at the edge of the rough. I lean against Dan's vehicle, shifting my weight to my right leg. I cannot imagine the frenzy of hatred that would drive someone to this extent.

Philip's drunken words of weeks ago grip my heart. He said Jobi would kill them both if she discovered their feelings for each other. Last night, she said, "Bill is gone." Was she trying to kill Marcy too, when she started the fire at the Wren?

Tom helps Dan take photographs of the grizzly scene, as I stand by and think minacious thoughts. Tom holds the tape while Dan measures the distance from the body to the golf club. Tom records the measurements then Dan carefully wraps white paper around the club and places it in the trunk of his cruiser.

The ambulance from Clark's Funeral Home arrives while they are working. After Dan has outlined the position of the body with lime from the grounds-keeper's shack, Bill's body is placed on the gurney and covered with a sheet.

We are tired and shocked by the brutality of the murder, but they continue the investigation to the best of their ability. They slowly walk in ever widening-circles around the green. The golf cart Harrington and Beckworth used is parked between the sandtrap and the gravel cart path. They find no extra tracks of either a cart or feet around the green. Tom takes a photograph of the fine line of sand across the green and the raked sandpit; the rake is lying on the right side of the trap.

Both Dan and Tom have reached the same conclusion.

Bill was killed somewhere else and placed on the golf course to be discovered by the first hapless twosome of players.

* * * * *

When I finally return to the house, Marcy is curled up on a sofa fast asleep. Her face is streaked with tears; the news had reached the diner that Bill was dead—murdered. It is pathetic that our phones do not work as well as the grapevine where bad news is concerned.

She is wrapped in my grandmother's afghan. A slight hiccup disturbs her quiet breathing. Watching her, I am astounded at the depth of her courage to withstand three devastating blows within twenty-four hours and still find solace in sleep.

Again I have nothing to offer in the way of comfort except my presence and love. What can I do to ease her pain when I am about to fall over my own feet from exhaustion? I leave her to the healing power of slumber and climb the stairs to my room to seek a few hours for myself.

The bang of the front screen door awakens me. It is nearly dark. I understand that she does not wish to show any of her pain to the curious. The lights from Marcy's car shine on the ceiling as she backs out of the drive. By the time I reach the window only the tail lights of the Lincoln glow as she rounds the corner.

Propped on my desk is her note:

Elton, I can't stay here. I've gone to Capital City
to replenish my wardrobe and get things for the
house. Don't worry, I will stay in a hotel. Running
away is not good but no matter how ill she is I can't

be responsible for what I might do. Wilson will
begin serving breakfast tomorrow.

* * * * *

The week has flown; I seldom see Marcy. She is living
in her cottage with little more than a camp cot and hot
plate. She refuses to come to town but I talk to her each
night. Between losing her few connections to Kira Lynn
and Bill on the same night, she has been shaken to the core.
It is one place where I will not tread until she indicates she
is willing to talk. I hate to see the silent grieving, it is as
though the storm of tears dried-out all personal feelings and
has left a shell of the woman.

Adam Young and his brothers are doing a great
remodeling job on the old place, but Marcy was
grateful the old privy was still standing while they
finished her bathroom and connected the new septic
system. The old one had proven to be a fifty-five-
gallon drum filled with gravel connected to the house
by tar-paper septic drain pipe. Tree roots had packed
the holes until it crumbled.

Next week she expects four rocking chairs and a swing
for the front porch, while for now she has a bedframe, but
no mattress. She delights in telling me where she found
each item. Old things from junk shops and antique stores
that correspond to the age of the house. Pieces she
remembers from her childhood when the world was safe. I
plan to give her my grandmother's afghan as a Christmas
and house-warming gift.

The debris from the Wren has been taken to the dump
and its site leveled. A few pieces of the willow china from
the dining room were salvaged to be sold later at an

auction. I try not to look at the vacant space between the alley and the bank by Esther Perkins' furniture store. A part of Clydsville heritage has been destroyed. It looms like an accusation of our carelessness with our past.

CHAPTER 13

When I reach the Kricket I regain my perspective on our future. The old diner is now the Knock Kneed Kricket Kafe, with paper napkins bearing the name and the most arrogant cricket ever to grace a serviette. He has a dash of sass that would give competition to a cockroach named *archy*.

The counter and stools have been re-chromed. Bright red cushions grace the stools. The high-backed booths are painted white, their seats are covered with the same fabric. We choose to sit at a long table in front of the window on chrome chairs upholstered in large red and white stripes.

An old iron corrugated radiator, rescued from Carl Andrews' junkyard, clunks along merrily, punctuated by intermittent hisses to provide the perfect degree of heat behind my back. The Kricket does not look as I remember it from childhood. The old diner was never this spotlessly clean or exuberantly gay.

The dishes are from the Homer Laughlin Company in West Virginia. Harry Bidwell talked Wilson into taking the heavy Fiesta with their brilliant colors off his hands. They had been sitting in his basement storeroom for nearly twenty years. A disastrous truckload purchase of his father-in-law's, which never sold, because after the war people did not want to be reminded of the deprivation of the 1930's.

A colorful way to start any morning. Mugs, cups, cream pitchers hang from shelves above the booths, the shelves are stacked with bowls, fat round canisters, teapots, pitchers, and vases. Platters of various sizes hang on the walls between the windows and doors.

Beside the coffee urn is a rack of pegs holding large white mugs for morning use. Tom Clement sits across from me wearing a sickening green bow tie with purple dots. He has not forgotten the promise he rashly made at the Wren. He is admiring his special mug: Bob Cratchit sitting humped over a tall desk, writing furiously with his quill pen. Mine has Ichabod Crane astride his fearful steed with legs dangling below the stirrups. Dan Sommers' has a sheriff's badge resting beside a tombstone.

When Cadel Beckworth and Gilbert Harrington come in they avoid our table to sit in the far back booth where no one can hear their conversation. Their mugs are plain white.

"Where were you yesterday?"

"Helping Marcy unpack kitchen fixings. She gave me her first dinner in the new place. Hamburgers and salad. Not bad." I grin, remembering the charred rocks, lost in the middle of a bun. We ate them anyway.

"Should have known. Well, you missed all the fun."

"What happened?"

"Philip. . . ."

"Philip? Is he all right?"

Dan looks at me with laughter in his eyes. "He's sleeping it off in jail. You can go over and post bail after we eat."

"Why is he in jail?"

"I had to charge him with DWI with two horses."

I remember him trying to be a circus performer. He almost broke his neck when he lost the reins.

"Dan, you are not making sense. Did he try to ride two horses?"

"Told you, you missed all the fun. Kathryn Burton has a fine temper. She pressed charges."

Their faces break into laughter, while I sit bewildered. They are behaving as if they have pulled off the coup of the century. In the kitchen both Wilson and Lon Chambers are laughing. Tom and Dan are waiting for me to play straightman.

"Kathryn Burton. What happened?"

"Philip was drunk and stole Kathryn's prize mare. Rode her into town barebacked, he was trying. . . ." Tom stops in the middle of his sentence to wipe his eyes. "To rope a parking meter. Kathryn had been to the bank and was walking back to the courthouse. Of course, the mare went to her and Philip roped Kathryn."

Dan Sommers takes up the tale, as Tom is laughing too hard. "Judge Burton was furious. Philip almost knocked her down besides stealing a mare-in-foal. She insisted I arrest him and charged him with horse stealing and driving while intoxicated. Don't have a law on the books for riding while drunk."

"Dan hitched the mare to the parking meter while Judge Burton called John Henry to bring a trailer into town to take her home. He made Philip put a quarter in the meter for a full hour."

"Oh, dear. I thought Philip was staying with Jobi?"

"No, Doc Flanders sent her home a few days ago. Emma Parker checks on her several times a day, but all she does is hold Little Bill, fondling him and calling him 'my little man.' That's the most anyone has heard her say since the Wren burned."

"Dan, you agreed to her release?" I am shocked. "We know she set the fire and killed Bill."

"She wasn't in custody. Elton, she didn't kill Bill."

"She didn't?"

"No, the state coroner put the time of Bill's death between one and three a.m. Bill died of asphyxiation."

"Asphyxiation? But the golf club."

"It wasn't the murder weapon. All it had on it was blood and a few hairs."

I am flabbergasted. "But his head?"

"Coroner says that was done after he died."

"After he died? But why?"

"Elton, I don't know. But Jobi couldn't have killed him. Tom found her behind the Wren about one-thirty. Emma Parker says her car was in the drive all night. The fire started around twelve-thirty, as near as we can tell. Everyone could see Bill's car. It was parked on the far side of the bank until Herman Geish towed it home the next day, after I examined it."

"Towed? Where were his keys?"

"Can't locate 'em.

"Anyway, she was with us when he died. I took her to the hospital with Philip. We can't even prove she actually set the fire though we can make a strong case. She had gasoline on Marcy's dress and the other clothes I found in the woods belonged to Marcy. They were soaked in gasoline, with the gas can beside them. Her fingerprints were all over the can."

"Then who killed Bill?"

* * * * *

"Elton, follow me to the jail. You've got to post bail for Philip. I can't go to Judge Burton and request she drop the charges."

"A couple of days locked up may do him some good."

"But it won't help Bill's little boy."

"Dan, he is with his mother."

"That's what I mean. Philip is Jobi Leighton's next of kin, isn't he?"

"Yes, I suppose so, now that Bill is dead."

"I didn't want to tell you in the Kricket, but Jobi Leighton is one sick woman. She needs help. It isn't right what's she's doing to that boy."

Dan's face is getting dusty red under his tan, he is trying to tell me something he does not want to say.

"Dan, what is wrong?"

He runs his left hand with the missing little finger through his hair, clearly hating what he perceives as a duty. "It isn't fitting. She. . .she holds him, fondling his privates until. . .he has an erection! Elton, he's less than four years old. Something's got to be done. I'd just gotten back from there when Philip pulled his stupid stunt."

"You were at their house?"

"Yeah." He grimaces like he has bitten into a sour pickle. "Emma Parker found them when she heard Little Bill crying and went over. She called me. I went out to investigate. The back door was standing wide-open for anyone to see. Managed to get the boy away from her. Emma took him next door.

"I called Opal, who got her dressed and stayed with her while I came back to find Philip. Opal spent the night, I told her she's still in shock from Bill's murder. Don't need this appalling story spread all over town. What are we going to do?"

"Get Philip out of jail. Their uncle lives in Cloverton. He took Jobi when their parents died, maybe he can take Little Bill until she is able to care for him properly." I am grasping at straws, but for this one, Philip had better be sober.

CHAPTER 14

Did you know your sister and my brother-in-law are taking my wife's parents to Florida for the holidays?"

"Yes, she told me. This time of year the skies cloud up and stay that way till March. They will enjoy the sun."

"But what are we going to do for Christmas dinner? We always go to Cloverton."

"Betty is a fine cook."

"You sound like your sister. When I mentioned it, she said it was time Betty and I start our own traditions, now that Aaron is five."

"Carolyn has a point; families should have customs."

"But we do have a custom, we go to Grandma's house for Christmas."

"Has fatherhood made you a sentimentalist?"

"A sentimental newspaper editor is an oxymoron." He huffs up and pats his mustache, which I refuse to mention. A scraggly patch of hair in the early stages of growing, it does not add a thing to his purple bow-tie persona.

"We do our family celebration on Christmas Eve. Betty didn't want him being fooled by the Santa Claus myth. It's too hard on children to discover that their parents lie to them."

Elroy is refilling our coffee cups while we wait for our breakfast. "Tom Clement, children need some fantasy to soften the blows life deals them. We're planning a fun day for Tal and Sunny. Stockings and all."

"Are you enjoying your new career?"

"It's temporary, until something in our line turns up. Must say though, Lon's gettin' to be a better cook, so it has its benefits. Some regulars don't leave much in the way of tips. Besides, Wilson insists we deposit them in Tal's piggybank." He points the coffee pot at a huge ceramic yellow pig sitting beside the brass Remington cash register. The pig sports a bright plaid bandanna around its neck, Marcy's scarf!

"Lon, bring your plate out here. We have a few minutes before people who don't arrive before the crack of dawn come in. Elroy, bring our cups and we'll eat." Wilson places eight full plates, a stack of hot biscuits and a bowl of gravy on the table before Dan Sommers makes it through the front door. I marvel at his ability to line plates up his arms and never drop one, a skill they must teach in cooking school.

The Kricket does not officially open until seven, but we have gotten in the habit of arriving about six-fifteen when Mese's shift ends. I can hear Tal coming down the stairs with slow steps as he holds Sunny's hand so she will not fall. Her goal is to be the first to open the backdoor for Mese.

Dan comes in the front as Marcy enters from the back, brushing light flakes of snow from her hair. Mese follows her like a courtlier of old following his queen. He bends to pick up Sunny, who immediately reaches for Marcy's hair.

"Shut the door, your breakfast is getting cold."

"Let us shed our coats and we'll be right with you. I'd forgotten snow. Look out the window." She takes Sunny and places her in the highchair between her chair and Mese's.

"Good morning Mr. Elton, Mr. Clement, Sheriff." Mese puts out his hand and gravely shakes each of our hands. Mese's delight in remembering each of our names has become a new custom since Wilson opened the diner. It is a pleasure to break our fast with friends and the children. The atmosphere is different from the Wren, more like a family meal.

"What were you talking about when I came in? It looked like a serious discussion."

I wink at Marcy. "It is serious; Tom's Christmas dinner is going south. He is being left to starve."

"What? Betty is one of the best cooks in Brewster County! Opal collects every recipe from the paper."

"But that is home-cooked food; I get it every night."

"Do I get to tell Betty what you just said about her cooking?"

"Elton Fightmaster! You know what I meant." His bow tie is wiggling as everyone erupts in laughter.

"I know how to solve his problem." Wilson's brown eyes dart around the room. "My grand opening will be Christmas Day. I'll fix stuffed goose with chestnut dressing and apples stuffed with sweet potatoes."

"Whoever heard of stuffing apples with sweet potatoes? You put raisins and butter in the core-hole of baked apples." Dan looks at me across the table, as if somehow I would know about cooking; all I know is about eating.

"It is an old southern dish, sprinkled with pecans."

"Betty will steal that recipe. It sounds good!"

"She's welcome to it."

"No, turkey is traditional." Tom looks shocked; he does not like change.

"In England and France it's a goose with Angels on Horseback on the side. Didn't have turkey until the Pilgrims settled in New England."

"Angels on Horseback? Wilson, I've seen a lot of horses but never saw no angel ridin' one."

"Elroy, he means, oysters wrapped in bacon and broiled. They are served with a hot mustard sauce. I had them in Scotland for one of their high teas at the hospital."

"They didn't serve me anything like that when I was in the hospital. Mostly gruel. Hated the stuff."

"Yes, the nurse told me about your bad manners." Lon holds his hand up to prevent Elroy from saying anything else in front of the children. "Wilson, are you serious?"

"Why not? You aren't doing anything special, are you?"

"No. We could bring you some fresh-caught trout from the river, though as Mr. Tom says, Christmas is for families."

"Lon, you're as bad a fuddy-duddy as Mr. Clement. Miss Betty's family is going to Florida, Elton's too. My sister is in New York and your family is in Minnesota. No one in this crowd will be with their families, so having the grand opening will work. Dress the fish; people down here don't care for dead eyes staring at them."

"I could bring. . . ."

"Wilson, stop calling me, Mr. Clement."

"Yes, sir."

"Marcy gal, you can make coffee."

"But. . . ."

"Don't allow women in my kitchen, you have other

87

talents but cooking isn't one of them."

Marcy's idea of a gourmet meal is opening a can of tuna fish. The Young twins swear they will never touch the stuff again.

"Tal, its time for you to get ready for school; the bus will be by any minute. Elroy, fix Mrs. Duncan a coffee, while I put a sausage in a biscuit for her."

* * * * *

Wilson solved Tom's holiday problem by declaring Christmas Day his official opening, with a traditional dinner. The ladies of Clydsville accepted with the provision they would be allowed to make a contribution.

Marcy and I were allotted the beverages. I suspect Elroy had contributed the information about her lack of culinary skills. To make the proper provisions, we take a trip to Capital City.

When I replace my Buick, I am going to get a Lincoln. It has the new style bucket seats on separate tracks, which accommodate my height quite comfortably.

With a profound look of satisfaction, Marcy surveys the backseat of the Lincoln piled high with gaily wrapped presents. "Elton, will there be room for us to drive home?"

"We'll squeeze in somehow." All of the packages are not hers; I have contributed my share after she explained to me the very real need for soft clothes for both Tal and Sunny. Their skin is still tender from the burns and, like all children, they are growing. Sunny's injuries are the most extensive and demand constant care for any sign of infection.

The doctors in Cincinnati have decided to wait before beginning skin grafts. As long as Mese is within her sight she has no fear of either doctors or hospitals. She has become Doc Flanders' pet with her constant chatter which, to me, is seldom understandable.

I started to purchase a Mammy ragdoll for Sunny but Marcy forbade my doing so. She had worked with the great character actress Hattie McDaniels and despised the caricature of her most famous role. Like everyone else, I had watched the voting and school integration struggle on television. Brewster County's Negro population has always been small, so it was like viewing something from a foreign country.

School integration for Brewster County was a necessity. The Negro high school was destroyed by a tornado. The county did not have the money to build a new one so all the students were sent to the central high school the same year of the Supreme Court decision which rocked the deep South.

An ancestress of Marcy's moved her slaves out west sometime in the 1820's. I accept her caustic evaluation of my ignorance of the complex issue. I cannot help but remember the Haskinses' prejudice, thinly disguised as welfare concern.

Sunny has long conversations with Marcy, which Marcy solemnly informs me are girl-secrets, not to be shared with men. Marcy's affection for the child is warm but does not fill the wound in her heart created by the loss of her own daughter. She never mentions Kira Lynn.

When Sunny is fast asleep in Marcy's arms, her tiny hand clasped tightly around a lock of Marcy's hair, I see Marcy gazing through the distance into to painful memory.

"What is that?"

She is pointing at Finder's World, a long row of buildings in the distance.

"A flea market."

"Elton, surely they don't sell fleas?"

"No, but they do sell just about everything else. Inside are partitioned spaces where people display their merchandise."

"Like a fair?"

"Yes."

"Do you mind if we stop?"

* * * * *

Marcy insists I get out by the entrance, and then parks the car as close to it as possible. A sharp wind cuts across the parking lot, pushing paper litter like a bulldozer. Her pale green silk-moire coat rustles like late fall leaves as she darts toward me, holding her hat against the wind. She changes the ribbon on the Mennonite hat to match whatever she is wearing. Today it is the yellow paisley of the lining of her coat. The black-framed square glasses are not part of an intentional disguise; Marcy is nearsighted.

Her eyes grow large with the wonder of a child as she studies the faux oriental rugs and banners hanging from the ceiling. She fingers piles of T-shirts and sweat shirts, but the deep, rich smell of leather draws her like a magnet. Her hand caresses the fine carving on the purses, but the rows of boots attract her favor.

The booth's occupant is a craftsman. His deeply wrinkled and tanned skin suggests a man who lives with the outdoors. They find a perfect fit for her in the wares for children and enjoy a fine haggle over the price. Marcy may never have seen a flea market but she has acquired great skill in the art of bargaining, which both parties enjoy.

We are sitting on wooden barstools, enjoying some

terrible coffee and eating cotton candy. I am lost, as I watch her tongue strip threads of the pink confection from the cone. Then the shrill shrieks of a violin being tuned shatters the spell.

In a booth across from where we perch, an old man is tinkering with the knobs of an ancient fiddle and listening to a pitch only he can hear. Three other men leave their stalls and take down instruments displayed on the walls.

Marcy watches each move they make. When they begin to play she silently claps her hands, unmindful of the sticky fluff endangering any passerby. I take the cone and she licks her fingers, but her eyes never leave the hands of the musicians as they fly across the strings.

I do not recognize one song, but I hear Marcy singing under her breath, "Sally in the garden, sifting sand/Sal's upstairs with a hog-eyed man."

She knows the words to nearly every song they play. For over an hour the old men play to the pretty girl enthralled by their unique style. The mountain sounds of the fiddle, guitar, banjo and mandolin bring the tinkling bells of laughter from her throat—a sound I haven't heard in a long time. She is lost to the voice of the music.

She pulls four business cards from her purse and swiftly writes across the back, 'Thank you! Marci Layne.' She had told me she no longer used the screen spelling of her name.

As the fiddler strikes a haunting, mournful tune, the other players set their instruments aside. Marcy sinks down on the floor, sitting cross legged, with tears streaming down her face. When he completes the number she silently gives each man one of her cards, unmindful of her tears. I follow her out of the flea market.

"What happened? You looked so happy."

"Women cry when they are happy. No, Elton, I won't

lie to you, the song was *Lost Girl*. I couldn't take it; I remembered so much. There is another one called, *Lost Boy*. I guess in the mountains, in the early days, it was easy for children to become lost in the woods and never be found, so they wrote songs about it to heal their grief."

"I am so sorry. What does a hog-eyed man look like?"

Just a giggle as she shakes a cigarette from the package but the tears have dried. "I have no idea. I don't think I was supposed to learn that one."

"The musicians were surprised you knew the words, I could tell by the looks on their faces. They were testing you. Where did you learn those songs? I did not know a one." I light her cigarette and one for myself, then she starts the car.

"When I was little, way before I started school, Aunt Cynthia would hitch up the wagon and take a load of food up the bank of the river to a long log building. I was never permitted to go in, because it was some kind of soldier's club; she fixed the food and they paid her. The most wonderful music would drift through the windows, and that was what we were hearing today. I'd never heard music except on the crank Victrola. We didn't have a radio because we didn't have electricity.

"Sometimes one of the soldiers would come out and wrap me in his great coat while Cynthia was inside. They would tell me the title of the songs and sing the words. I loved the funny ones like, *Old Hen Crackled*, *Indian ate the Woodchuck*, and *Big Eared Mule*.

"One soldier gave me his knife when they played *Barlow Knife*. He said he was going far away and might lose it. Aunt Cynthia took it away from me. But she allowed me to keep *Polly Grand*, my kitten. I named her after one of the songs, but she had to live in the barn."

The mischievous giggle again as she stubs out the

cigarette. "Polly was actually a big orange male. He always found my pillow before morning. Drove her crazy trying to figure out how he got back in the house. We never did know, but I'd wake up with him purring beside me and feel safe."

I remember how the fellas talked in awed whispers about the log barn of a house on the river that catered to the needs of the military during the war. It was the last building torn down before the water was impounded for the lake. Miss Cynthia delivering food to a bordello with Marcy in a wagon is hard to comprehend.

* * * * *

"Where do children get so much energy?"

"Elton, it is time you had some of your own, then you would know the answer."

"How many times did I read *The Little Engine That Could*?"

"Never seen Aaron remain still for so long. It was a good choice for a Christmas present. One I think my son will remember it for a longtime."

Elroy eases into the chair next to me. "It's peaceful when the kids are on vacation. They spent the night at Marcy's. I heard a Clem joke, not proper for mixed company.

"Clem took his grandfather to see Doc Flanders for a checkup. The old man must be pushin' ninety. Doc is doin' his probin' and listenin', when he starts askin' questions:

"Mr. Claymore, do you smoke?"

"Nope, can't afford nothin' but corn-shucks. Taste terrible."

"Doc listens again, does more pokin'. 'Mr. Claymore, do you drink?'

"Nah, Sidmore's stuff'll corroded your innards."

"Concerned Doc puts his ear to the old man's chest, 'I hear a heart murmur. Do you have a sex life?'

"Yes, you sneak. It's what you get for listenin' where you ain't supposed to. I'm lookin' at your wife and rememberin'."

The back door bangs, "Elroy! You're telling a dirty joke."

"Marcy gal, you were eavesdropping with children present. Shame on you."

"Mr. Elton, will you read. . . ."

CHAPTER 15

"Elton, you blessed man. How did you do it?"

Miss Edith Bradley is a distant cousin of my mother's. As I enter the bank, she is coming out. She greets me with fond enthusiasm while talking non-stop, ignoring the question she has asked.

"Elton, I just knew when you became a member of the board here at the bank you would do something about the poor dividends we get on our savings."

"Miss Edith, I have not. . . ."

"You are being modest. Pauline Cross, Esther Perkins, and Mildred Osborne all called me. They are delighted, after losing everything in the fire, to see a bigger dividend. So I drove into town and my dividend has increased."

She is pointing inside the bank as I hold the door for her. "That nice man over there behind the counter looked it up on their books. Pauline, Esther, and Mildred have taken rooms with Beatrice Carstairs but they need clothes and fixings. Thank you, thank you."

She waves her hand and crosses the street, heading for

the Carstairs' home. She never gave me a chance to tell her I did not know about a raise in dividends. The man she indicated is standing behind Calvin Forkes, who has been head teller for the bank since I can remember.

I assume he will be replacing Bill Leighton as the assistant manager and is showing the stranger his duties.

Mr. Forkes looks up at me over his half-rimmed glasses with grateful eyes, as if I have rescued him from drowning. "Mr. Stolmeyer, Elton Fightmaster can help you. Mr. Fightmaster is the president of our board of trustees.

"Elton, Mr. Alfred Stolmeyer is with the State Bank Examiner's office." His fragile voice shakes as he explains the situation. "We have a problem with the dividends paid on savings accounts." The man I am facing has a granite countenance without the least shadow of tolerance.

"We do! Where is Cadel Beckworth? I do not know anything about the day-to-day operation of the bank."

"He had a meeting in Capital City today. Please Elton, help Mr. Stolmeyer. Bill Leighton always took care of the dividend payments and he's dead. I've shown him the records. We have customers, and Miss Feishter does not come in when Mr. Beckworth is out of the office. I am alone."

Forkes' desk is piled with bank bags from the night depository. Currency, coins and checks are stacked by a deposit book. He has been so busy handling customers and Mr. Stolmeyer's requests, he has not had the time to finish the night deposits. Stacks of folders are resting on the corner of the crowded desk.

I glance behind me, and see that a line is forming. Each person is holding their bank book tightly clasped in their hands. I have no choice. I had let myself be elected president of the board as a rank newcomer, the reasoning being that I live closest to the bank. Faced with the stern visage of the state official, it seems a poor rationality. He reminds me of my father.

"Mr. Forkes, has every bank customer who has come in this morning experienced the same pleasant surprise?"

"Yes, sir."

"You need help. Call Miss Feishter. Tell her I requested she come to work today to help you."

"Yes, sir."

Stolmeyer is looking grimmer, but has not said a word. I force a smile in his direction. "As Mr. Forkes has explained, he has duties to the bank customers, so let us adjourn to Mr. Beckworth's office. This way, please."

I open the door and stand back to let him precede me into the crowded room. A small moan escapes his lips, "There isn't any place to work in this mess."

Beckworth's office is even worse than usual. He has been moving all the furniture around. The big table that was by the wall is now in front of the windows, and more chairs are crowded around it. It is sitting on an area rug overlapping the oriental carpet, which covers the floor vents. The room is cold and stuffy at the same time, with an odd odor, something like corroded copper mixed with stale cigar smoke.

His desk is beside the table, making opening the door a hazard. Tall gun-metal filing cabinets line the wall where the table once stood. I agree with Mr. Stolmeyer; there is no adequate space in which to work.

"Do you have a portable adding machine?"

He gives me a strange look. "Yes."

"Is it within the law for you to leave the premises when doing an examination?"

"Rather unusual, but I'm unaware of any regulation to the contrary."

"Good. My office is around the corner behind the post office. I suggest we take the savings account files and work there."

The furnace gives a loud belch, sending more carpet fumes into the packed space. "Mr. Fightmaster, I appreciate your suggestion and will be glad to accept."

* * * * *

Stolmeyer and I work until late in the evening. I call Wilson, who sends Elroy to deliver a superb *Beef Bourguignonne* over egg noodles for dinner. Even in my own home, under the circumstances, I offer Stolmeyer tea as a beverage, though I have a young burgundy I want to try.

The results of our endeavors point directly to a full audit of all the bank's records. We use my old bank books as a sample, matching entries against the account sheets. Almost ten years ago, someone within the bank had started shorting the savings accounts by one percent a month, a small amount that was not noticeable as it followed a withdrawal of funds.

It is a very clever scheme. A customer makes a withdrawal from their account, and from that point to the present the interest paid is reduced by one percent. In my own account, with compound interest, it amounts to more than a thousand dollars. I am staggered when I do a little mental arithmetic against the number of passbook-savings accounts serviced by the bank.

Bill Leighton's death precipitated the disaster when Mr. Forkes assumed his duties and figured the current period's interest at the standard three percent. The monies must be repaid when the final audits expose the extent of the theft.

How will I be able to face people, accepting their undeserved thanks and appreciation for their windfalls, when I know the magnitude of the fraud?

Stolmeyer is very fastidious. He gathers up every piece of tape from his machine and mine, which he then has me initial. He packs them along with the bank records in the large bank bag we obtained from Calvin Forkes. The only positive comment he makes is to the quality of the waterproof lining of the bank bag. Then he thanks me for dinner and departs.

This leaves me with the dubious pleasure of informing Beckworth of the state of the fraud, and Stolmeyer failed to mention when to expect the state auditors to arrive. To prevent a panic among the depositors, he did suggest that nothing be said pending the outcome of their investigation.

As president of the board will I be held responsible for negligence or worse, complicity? I could lose my license to practice law.

* * * * *

"You look wretched." Tom's candor about my appearance after a night of walking the floor is galling. He's wearing a pink bowtie, and his father's old tweed jacket almost drags the floor.

"I can say the same for you."

"Worried about that business at the bank yesterday?"

"I spent the evening with Mr. Stolmeyer doing a few of the accounts, including my own. The fraud has been going on for a long time. Cadel Beckworth is not expected back until tomorrow, and Stolmeyer left me the duty of informing him of the facts before the State brings down the formal indictment against the bank and its officers. All of the accounts are frozen as of this morning, until a full formal audit can be completed."

"How are we going to conduct business?"

"Excuse me, I am tired. I misled you. The savings accounts are frozen, not personal or business accounts. No, Elroy, I do not need any more coffee."

"Fruit jars will be coming out of the woods."

"What are you talking about?"

"Before you were born, Dan. People still remember when the banks closed and they couldn't get their money. Prudent folks still keep a deposit buried for a rainy day."

Tom's pencil is flying across the page. "What?"

"Now don't you go printing that. This is a private conversation."

"Elroy, you were eavesdropping on a private conversation."

His green eyes gleam as if he has discovered three nitwits. "You all are the only customers. Wasn't hard." He stands his ground, looking down at us like a schoolmaster. "If you put that in the paper, the hardware store won't have enough shovels. What are you goin' to put in the paper?"

"This is the biggest bank heist we have had since Jessie James robbed the bank in Creelsboro. I have to report it."

"See my point? People don't trust banks. More than a hundred years it's been goin' on. The Union boys were fine fellas but they helped themselves to anythin' they could lay a hand to. Boys in butternut goin' back across the line did the same. Folks have good reason to be cautious."

Lon appears by Elroy's elbow, "I need your help." He is looking at Elroy but his black eyes take in the entire table; his face is drawn and grave.

"Sure."

Lon points vaguely to the wall phone. "My sister just

called. My father has died, they need me at home. Will you help me drive?"

Elroy reaches for his friend, as we sit stunned, not knowing what to say. They turn to go out the backdoor. Wilson throws them the keys to the Aston Martin. "Don't worry about anything here; we'll take care of it. Let me know when you get there; call collect. Where do we send flowers?"

A small chuckle escapes Lon, "They would freeze in the delivery truck. Put your money in the college fund and thanks. We will be careful with the car."

CHAPTER 16

I follow the pounding on the front door through the house, being careful not to drop mud on the carpet.

"Sheriff, I am sorry. I was in the garden, I did not hear your car."

"Elton, that isn't important. Harrington made me arrest Marci Layne."

"What? Why?" Sommers' face is red and streaks of sweat run down his neck under his collar. His breathing is heavy as if he has run over here instead of driving—he *has* run; only my Buick is in the driveway.

"I didn't want to, but I have my sworn duty. You've got to get her out. Post bail. She didn't kill Bill Leighton, no matter what the little evidence we have says."

"You've arrested Marcy for Bill's murder!"

"She told me to get you. I came right away." He raises his hand to brush his cornsilk hair back from his face. Dark stains ring the tan of his uniform shirt under his arms on this the third day of February.

"Where is Marcy?"

"She is in a cell; couldn't leave her in the office while I ran over here. Harrington will have my job. She's under arrest. He's in the courthouse trying to get Judge Morgan to hold a preliminary hearing to see if. . . ."

"Dan, I know what happens in a preliminary hearing. She must be represented by counsel. Go back to Marcy. I'll be there as soon as I change shoes."

I clean up in the kitchen and drive to the Sheriff's office. Gilbert Harrington is trying to question Marcy. She sits slumped in a chair, ignoring him as he paces around the small room. She is wearing her blue jeans and an extra large plaid shirt, both are spotted with pink dots. There are black streaks across her forehead and nose. She is trying to pull a bright blue rubber glove off her right hand through the handcuffs while holding the cuff of the other glove in her teeth.

"Elton, I was cleaning windows. He. . . ." she stammers. She is shaking her hands at Harrington with the pink traced glove like a gauntlet to toss in his face.

"Came with Sheriff Sommers and demanded that I get in the car. He wouldn't allow me to get my purse. He's had me arrested for killing Bill." Whimsical strands of red-gold are escaping from the rubber band at the back of her head like storm signal flags .

Harrington is from Buckston, on the other side of the county. He is too confirmed in his own self-righteousness to recognize Marcy's temper.

"Marcy, this is a mistake. I will get it straightened out and take you home. . .to finish the windows. Dan, take those cuffs off her. Are you hurt? What is on your face and your clothes?"

"No. I don't know. Elton, for your edification you use Glass Wax, which is pink, to clean windows, then you polish it off with old newspaper. I must have smeared the *Banner*s' ink on my face. They don't provide mirrors in police cars."

Harrington looks at her in awe and sucks in his stomach, "Miss Layne, you're not going anywhere. You're under arrest by the sovereign state of. . . ."

"Gilbert, we are a Commonwealth, not a state."

"Fightmaster, I know that."

"I did not want you to make another mistake. One a day is all we are allowed."

"Are you her attorney?" I nod. "If so, then you know the law. No matter who she is, she is not going home and clean windows. She has been charged with first-degree murder."

"As her attorney, I am posting bail."

"You can't do that until after the preliminary hearing, which is tomorrow morning. Until then she remains in jail."

Sheriff Sommers is no innocent to the Lane temper and he stands with his back blocking the door to prevent the curious from entering. "Mr. Harrington, we don't have facilities for keeping a lady, never had one before."

"Sommers, I've had to explain to you before your oath in this matter."

Dan indicates to the two cells behind his desk. "We don't have any place for them to take care of their privates." His blush extends past the fading tan line across his forehead.

Harrington looks at him in confusion. I see my chance, "Sheriff, you will drive Miss Layne to my office so I can have a conference with my client. You can post a guard outside my home, which is the only decent place she can stay until the hearing." I pray my Gilbert Harrington pompousness is strong enough to get her out of the jail before she is guilty of murdering him. I have no real authority and all concerned know it.

"Fightmaster, you can't remove an accused murderess from custody."

"Mr. Harrington, do you have a better solution to your dilemma?" I take Marcy's elbow and usher her toward the door held open by Sheriff Sommers.

"My client would appreciate it if this fiasco goes no further; we will be having dinner at the country club tonight. Harrington, if you are nervous about her absconding before morning, a chair will be available outside her door for your convince."

* * * * *

When we enter the house, Marcy immediately assumes command of the situation, dismissing Harrington's allegations as preposterous. She refuses to consider the severity of his accusations. She is not about to let me ask any of the questions raging in my mind—the most important being, where was she the night of the fire?

I try to make her understand that I am not qualified to render assistance in a criminal trial, though I know several who can serve. I am a civil lawyer who does deeds, title checks, and maintains a few small trusts. I have seldom been in a court except for estate hearings. Murder is not a frequent event in Brewster County, and I have avoided the proceedings of the few trials.

I start to explain the purpose of the preliminary hearing.

"Elton, I did not kill Bill. I wasn't anywhere near town when he was killed. I couldn't sleep and. . .went for a drive along the river. I've told you before."

She had not; the only answer she had given me was, "making coffee."

"Marcy, what evidence does Harrington have that precipitated your arrest?"

"Dan said my finger prints were on the murder weapon. I told you about Bill showing me his golf club. Remember, Jobi took it and shoved it back in his bag."

"But that was months ago, when you first came home. How did Harrington get your fingerprints for a match?"

"How would I know? Off a glass at the Kricket maybe." She sinks down on the sofa and pulls a lock of hair around, twirling it though her fingers, like Sunny. "I don't understand it either, but that is the only time I ever touched that club. I haven't played golf, not once, since I arrived.

"I'm sorry, I'm rambling. That bird-brained nincompoop, he's trying to use my name. Wouldn't even let me take off the rubber gloves before he forced Dan Sommers to put me in cuffs. Did he think Tom Clement would be waiting at the jail with a camera for a front page splash?"

"Tom would not do something that vulgar."

"I know. I'm so tired." She lays her head back on the sofa and closes her eyes. Marcy's face is pale against the flame of her hair. She is not wearing makeup. The skin below her eyes is tinged with blue shadows. I want to pull her into my arms and hold her safe.

"Fix some coffee; I need a drink." Her voice comes from a distance between clinched teeth.

"I have some brandy."

"No, coffee. I must think. I should've done this weeks ago. Make a large pot. I won't attempt to escape; don't believe I could make it to the front door." Her eyes flutter open for a moment, then Marcy is asleep.

How can she do it, relax and fall asleep in the face of adversity?

* * * * *

Marcy refuses to consider the charge as anything more than Gilbert Harrington's grandstand play to get his name in the papers a few weeks after entering office.

Her story remains the same, she went for a drive along the river, didn't notice any other car until she was returning to town and saw the flames against the night sky. Racing to town, she nearly ran into the back of Lon Chamber's truck as he pulled into the parking lot of the Kricket. Elroy was with him.

She followed them into the restaurant and stayed to help Wilson prepare coffee, putting together rough sandwiches for the firefighters, and then helped him load his car. She stayed at the Kricket preparing more sandwiches and coffee. Then they brought the last load of food to town in his car.

She knew she did not have the strength to watch her life's funeral pyre. The hotel had held all of her possessions. She refused to give a personal display of hysterias in public. To protect herself she had to stay away until there was nothing left to burn.

Lon and Elroy are in northern Minnesota, which has been hit by a major snow storm, so they cannot verify her story. It is much too weak to present to Judge Morgan to obtain a dismissal of the absurd charges.

Tom Clement and Dan Sommers forestalled the lurid photo session of her humiliation. Dan took her into the jail by the backdoor over Harrington's protest. Tom, after receiving a call from Harrington prior to the arrest, had gone out to photograph a two-headed calf at a farm on the other side of the lake.

I make my calls from the kitchen to allow her to rest,

while I attempt to get a gag order to prevent Harrington from making any more public announcements.

Silas Morgan, our local circuit judge, is most helpful with a promise to prevent any unwarranted publicity, pending the outcome of the hearing.

* * * * *

The remainder of the afternoon is dedicated to personal business, Marcy has said all she means to say in regard to the hearing. I think back to the night she returned; there are canyons in Marcy that can not be breached. Terror rides every nerve that I will prove as inadequate in her defense as I have been to assuage her grief.

She instructs me to make her will, with Miss Cynthia as administratrix and myself as trustee and executor, for her daughter with the provision that if she is not located by the time of Miss Cynthia's death, the estate will in its entirety go to Miss Cynthia's next of kin.

As she gives me her deeply considered instructions, she tells me the story of her marriage and the loss of her daughter. Kira Lynn Endicott had been lost when Marcy's husband removed her from their California home prior to the divorce proceedings. Jeremy Endicott's car was smothered in an avalanche near the Nevada border. His body was found by the door. The authorities theorized that if he had stayed in his car he would have survived.

His mother denied all knowledge of her granddaughter and blamed Marcy for her son's death. She was furious with her son for making an ordinary will under which all his assets went to Marcy as his wife. She fought to have the will set aside because of the pending divorce at the time of his death, but it was declared valid, as his death occurred prior to the hearing.

They had a small vacation home in northern Colorado, but when she went there, Marcy discovered it had been destroyed. The human remains found in the fire-gutted structure were of a man and a woman, first identified as the owners, but later recognized as the caretaker and his wife. No remains of a child were found.

CHAPTER 17

The hearing is a disaster. The blood, small particles of skin, and two short hairs on the nine-iron are Bill's. Fingerprints taken from the shank and one thumb print on the grip are Marcy's.

It is obvious Bill Leighton had been struck with the club, but it was not the cause of death. Bill died of suffocation, according to what Dan Sommers had told me at the Kricket before Marcy was arrested. Harrington does not mention this during the hearing as he presents his evidence. Under the law I can only present rebuttal to disclosures made during the hearing by the prosecution.

When questioned by Sheriff Sommers, Mike Parker, the night-clerk from the Wren, stated that Marcy left the hotel nearly every night between ten and eleven. She did not return until about daylight each morning as his shift was ending. She had not mentioned her nightly wanderings to me, nor was she questioned with regard to this behavior by the Sheriff. The only frame of reference I have are old movie-magazine stories that tell of the same behavior after her daughter disappeared.

The accused does not have a voice in a preliminary hearing. Her initial statement is read by Dan Sommers. She sits beside me, her face devoid of expression, looking past the judge's shoulder at the map of Brewster County before the dam was built behind the podium. She has no alibi for the time of Bill's death, no one had seen her or her car until she arrived at the Kricket.

The hearing is held to establish the fact there is enough evidence for Gilbert Harrington to hold Marcy Lane for trial in the death of Bill Leighton.

He wins his motion to hold the trial beginning on Monday, as Mrs. Endicott is not a resident of Brewster County and therefore a good candidate to flee the state. I manage to meet the bail of fifty thousand dollars cash bond with a cashier's check provided by Wilson, and assure Judge Morgan that Marcy will remain in Brewster County.

Sheriff Sommers states for the court record, at her own request, that the defendant, Marci Layne will be housed at the home of Mrs. Beatrice Carstairs until the trial and that his office has impounded her car.

Judge Morgan refuses to lift the gag order, sidetracking any attempt of Harrington's to use the trial as a vehicle for his aspirations. It is a small margin of comfort that Marcy will be living across the square, because now she must be escorted to the jail or my office for any conferences.

Tom Clement follows the court documents hiding her identity behind her legal name, Margery Lynn Lane Endicott. The *Banner* prints only the bare facts in a small column as if they are of no importance, obeying the Judge's order to the letter, and effectively blocking Harrington's access to a wider media.

In retaliation for being denied statewide and national

publicity, Harrington uses every method he can devise to impede my contact with my client. Notwithstanding her posted bond, she is in essence under house arrest, even her meals are to be brought to the Carstairs home.

Marcy's own stubborn refusal to confide in me or expand on her initial statement leaves me to construct a weak defense. There is so much I do not know, I am forced to speculate or retreat into rebuttal in the face of Harrington's presentation. I will be working from a defensive position with no offense.

Saturday night I go into my parents' bedroom and looked across the square at the light in the room Marcy has been given, with a slight hope of inspiration. Her shadow passes the window, a vague phantom of the woman I love and have sworn to defend. My vibrant Marcy has fled, and only an impenetrable shell remains. It is as if she has lost the desire to live.

Calvin Forkes and Raymond Clark both arrived at the country club as Marcy was leaving. Cadel Beckworth maintains he did not actually witness Jobi Leighton remove the club from Marcy's hand, but he volunteer to serve as a defense witness. This leaves only Marcy's own statement as to when she handled the club.

Beckworth stops by our table for any news of developments in the case. He does not mention the missing money or the pending audit. Dan Sommers has to remind him that we are all bound until the trial by Judge Morgan's order not to discuss the case.

Wilson can support Marcy's story from the point she arrived at the Kricket behind Lon and Elroy. His help will be invaluable; his story places Marcy at the Kricket by three-thirty. Her car was still parked behind the restaurant when we arrived for breakfast after the fire. He does not know the cornoner's results.

No one has come forward to report seeing either her or the Lincoln for the crucial period when Bill died, which leaves a gap of an hour and a half.

Marcy's Lincoln is clean. Dan found fingerprints on the cigarette lighter and around the passenger seat but they proved to be mine. Is it enough to stave off Harrington's prosecution? I know she did not kill Bill Leighton, but the law demands proof of her innocence. Marcy loved Bill—a fact he cannot know.

* * * * *

I am starting up the stairs. I do not want to hear the soft knock on the front door; it has been a terrible day of useless speculation. Dan Sommers' car parked in front of Beatrice Carstairs' house draws my eyes to the light in Marcy's room, which flickers and goes out.

Two strangers stand under my porch light; one is wearing a white collar and the other a yarmulke. They are about the same height, below six feet.

"We know it's late, but may we come in? Wilson sent us to you."

"Of course, you are his brother-in-law?" I said turning to the rabbi.

A soft chuckle, "No. My name is Benjamin Lehman, I am Marcy's agent and a rabbi. I think it is called moonlighting but I've never been sure on which side of the fence. The Monsignor here is one of the high priests; he doesn't have to feed himself and a family."

"Mr. Fightmaster, may we explain?"

I flip on the lights in my office and indicate the couch. "Please do. Would you like a drink?"

"A brandy would be appreciated. It was a long flight, and Wilson's car is cramped."

The priest stretches his legs and I think of the Aston Martin two-seater. I am liberal with the beverage. Fine threads of grey in their dark brown hair tell me they are of the same age as Elroy and Lon.

"Please accept my apology, Ben introduced himself. I am J. Bryan Stanley; we are friends of Elroy Harris and Lon Chambers. We served with them in North Africa. Lon called us when his father died. We received a short-wave message from Elroy demanding that we get here to help Marcy, as they are snowbound."

I twirl the balloon glass in my hands, watching the thick liquid swirl and slide down the sides. Soft blue eyes and dark brown orbs study my face.

"Help Marcy? How?"

"We're not sure. As I said, we talked to Elroy by short-wave radio, and the reception was not good. Have you ever tried to dissuade him from any action?"

I have to smile, remembering the fruitless endeavors of the past two days. "Elroy, no—but Marcy, yes."

Monsignor Stanley grins back, "They do have traits in common. Marcy is an obsession with Elroy. He'll move mountains to protect her, but for the time being the snow has him flummoxed."

"I doubt it. My guess is he has Lon's entire family out digging with shovels."

"He wouldn't. It's twenty below up there. They live near the north side of Lake Superior."

"Of course he would. The lake must not be frozen enough for him to walk across. We're tired and Mr. Fightmaster needs our help. Elroy will get home when he can, and we are here."

Rabbi Lehman answers my original question. "We can testify as to her character. Bryan, like you lawyers, is bound by conventions of his calling but I'm not. We have known Marcy since she first came to California. Bryan arranged her living quarters when she arrived."

"The last time I saw her was the night we walked off the stage after our graduation ceremony. When did she go to California?"

"Shortly after that. She had been ill, but wanted to be an actress. Elroy and Lon sent her to us. She was lovely, with a raw talent, but no training. They helped her financially while she studied and practiced her craft in summer stock and little theater performances. Three years later I managed to obtain a screen test, which is difficult for an unknown, who refuse to become a blonde."

I can hear the smile in his voice, I am well acquainted with Marcy's obstinate character once she reaches a decision.

"While she was learning, she lived with the Holy Sisters."

"Marcy lived in a convent?"

"Yes, at Elroy's insistence. Once her career was established, she bought a small home near the beach, away from the city."

"Marcy spent most of her days at the studio, very little actual social life except when the studio demanded it for publicity. The image of the rising star flitting gaily about Hollywood is a false one, created for public consumption. It was the part of the business she hated—until she met Jeremy Endicott."

I believed every word printed in the magazines and newspapers. I am bedaze to learn of the myth. I have known this woman all my life, I understand her deep streak of privacy. I was proud to have known her, and 'there are fools such as I.'

"The marriage was doomed from the beginning. Endicott married the star, not the woman. He gloried in her fame but didn't understand the demands on her time that were necessary for her to remain a star. He wanted her for himself and set about to change the woman into the image."

"What do you mean? He did not hurt her, did he?"

"No, not physically, but he undermined her confidence in herself. I'm not making myself clear. The public sees a polished production, a story brought to life but making films is hard, grueling work."

"Demands? I do not understand."

"A working actress's day begins about 4:30 in the morning. She must be rested, there isn't time to party until the wee hours and work. Marcy made eight films in which she had the lead in less than ten years. The only time she took off was to have Kira Lynn.

"Watch *Silence*; many of the shots of Marcy are from the back, or head shots. Pregnant women don't make convincing romantic heroines. The agony she endured in tight corsets was what earned her the Oscar nomination; it bled through on film."

"Ben, Mr. Fightmaster has a long day tomorrow. We will go with him to escort Marcy to the courthouse."

"One question. Why did Marcy leave California?"

The expression in Monsignor Stanley's eyes is sad as he looks at me. "We don't know."

"On her last picture she complained of being tired all the time. She'd fall asleep in her chair waiting for the shooting to start. We assumed it was from her midnight forays running from the grief of losing Kira Lynn. I convinced her to see a doctor."

"She managed to finish the picture. Then two or three weeks later she walked into my rectory and told me she must go home. I assumed her aunt was ill and that she would return."

"By that time she had settled Endicott's estate, sold her property and liquidated her assets. The car was packed when she came to my office. I couldn't hold her; she never had a formal contract. As Bryan told you, we don't know, but it was like losing our own daughter. Elroy doesn't know either, I called him before she had cleared the city limits."

They pick up their coats and start toward the door. "You can stay here."

"That isn't necessary, we're staying on the houseboats."

"The houseboats?"

"Mr. Fightmaster, we've been to Brewster County many times. Priests and rabbis take vacations. Your fishing is wonderful and the Cumberland River is as close to God as a human can expect to live."

As I walk them to the door, I realize that Marcy and I have another common link: early morning rituals are no strangers in our lives.

CHAPTER 18

4:30 a.m. I am greeted by the alarm and the pains of the night. I must exercise my left leg with the precision of a ballet dancer's last call. My mind digs deep into my physique and urges individual muscles to respond. I can allow no other thoughts to invade the process until the ritual is complete.

After much pleading with the unresponsive limb, the shrunken tendons uncurl from their reflexive reaction to being free of the brace that holds them in captivity during the daylight hours. I push until they stretch and I can tell my toes to move. Every morning of my life I have envied friends who can hop out of bed and walk free to the bathroom.

My bedroom is both a sanctuary and a prison. I never allowed myself the luxury of screaming against the pain since the night Father caught me crying in my sleep. For months after the incident I lay awake, afraid to go to sleep, when my limb might betray me to his ridicule and contempt.

I ease my leg to the floor and grasp the rungs of the walker, pushing it before me like a grocery cart. The distance to the shower is but a few feet, yet it entails the most difficult steps I take in a day. I must not permit myself the extravagance of hopping on my right foot but plant each sole firmly on the floor, willing myself to move.

The searing water cascades against me as the frigid muscles continue to relax. The scars from innumerable operations dance like ropes of puckered ribbon on a Maypole in celebration of my victory over my own body.

I grasp the edge of the shower door and step over to a high stool, and lift my leg to wrap it in hot towels like a denizen in a Turkish bath for more of the precious heat to lengthen my disease-shortened muscles. The hour-long treatment of hot towels is followed by the probing of my fingers as they anoint each muscle in the thigh, knee, calf, and foot with warm oil, much as I imagine Jim Young lubricates his engines before a race. But Jim's work is intermittent while mine is daily and keeps me from inhabiting a wheelchair as did President Roosevelt.

* * * * *

Father would accused me of playing the fool, but I cannot allow the world to see a cripple defending Marcy. I drive my Buick around to the jail and park in front. A State policeman is escorting her down the steps as I arrive. They wait patiently until I get out. I leave my cane. I will walk with her.

Monsignor Stanley and Rabbi Lehman arrive with Wilson. Wilson, in a formal Brooks Bothers business suit is guaranteed to strike a chord of envy in Harrington's clothes-conscious breast.

Her cheeks glow against the wind. Winter has sucked the warmth from the sun. It is a cold, damp, thirty-two degrees. The early morning drizzle has ceased, but the dreary overcast claims the skies and invades my soul.

I smile at her, so brave wearing a silk-dress the color of the wet spring lichen on the trees topped by a boxy waist-length jacket. Her flaming hair is covered by a matching scarf almost like the snoods my mother wore. As we walk, I can hear the soft swish of her skirt and the sharp click of her heels on the old brick. She doesn't say a word but looks straight ahead.

Our entourage falls in behind us. The officer walks beside Wilson, who elected to carry my briefcase, clearly stunned by the ecclesiastical honor guard.

As we climb the courthouse steps, each riser gets higher. I am forced to pause to ease a dragging foot. The routine is automatic and I am thrilled that only Tom Clement waits with his camera at the top. The trial is here and I have no idea how to present her defense. I watched every episode of *Perry Mason* but it ceased four years ago.

"I did not kill Bill Leighton."

I have her word. It is enough.

CHAPTER 19

The heating system is working overtime. The courtroom is packed and smothering. Someone has opened the windows to allow a modicum of air to circulate through the heavy atmosphere. The odor of dry-rot pervades the heavy air. The windows need new frames. Marcy is seated to my left, closest to the open window. I hope she does not get chilled, but her jacket should protect her.

Witnesses are not allowed in the court until they are called, but Tom Clement has laid his overcoat across one row to save seats for the clergy and Wilson after their testimony. The jury box is empty. Oh dear! In my pondering of Marcy's defense I have forgotten the selection of the jury.

I look at her in dismay. How could I have been so stupid not to have checked with Maud Tosh as to who has been called to report to jury duty?

The trial has begun.

Judge Morgan speeds the selection along unwilling to

allow Gilbert Harrington time to access a phone and announce to the world that he has Marci Layne, the movie star, on trial for murder.

I manage to keep the Ladies Auxiliary off the jury but have to settle for Emma Parker and Odessa Haskins, two lone women seated with ten men, of whom Delbert Singleton and Alvin Carstairs are the best selections.

Harrington demonstrates his rhetoric in a booming voice that awakens Kyle Lefter. I suspect Lefter is still drunk, as he is leaning against the edge of the jury box rubbing his eyes.

His opening covers the brutality of the crime and catalogs Bill's contributions to the community. He pulls heart strings as he describes Jobi and Little Bill being deprived of a husband and father. He announces that he will prove beyond a shadow of a doubt that Margery Lynn Lane Endicott had a strong motive for murder.

I have a narrow margin of comfort. Harrington seems to love a good show where his harangue will be heard. He does not like the drudgery of homework. The broad picture of grieving family is his forte, with minor details a hindrance and of mundane composition.

The pile of papers before me is pitifully small. My job must be to take careful note of every piece of evidence he presents. I have no offense, except a polygraph test which is rather new. Marcy passed with flying colors—she knew nothing of the murder as she has maintained. Harrington was present when it was administered and will not refer to it.

Harrington intends to use Marcy as his ticket to Capital City. Dan Sommers is accurate in his assessment; Gilbert is afflicted with grandeur disease. The brown paper sleeve carefully restored, his copy of *Gentleman's Quarterly* is passed around the post office before being delivered to his office.

I object to the most flagrant and grandiose statements as is customary, but I am watching the jury and their eyes are glazed in boredom.

Judge Morgan makes impatient gestures and glances at the clock. He wants to get all of the technical testimony on the record before breaking for lunch, which will be short. He intends to prevent any reporters or a television news teams from reaching Brewster County before the close of the court session for today.

My opening statements are brief, little more than stating that Mrs. Endicott did not kill William Curtis Leighton. The undercurrents in the room swim in the heat. How has Harrington offended Judge Morgan? Whatever exists between them works to my advantage, and I am not my father's son for nothing.

Dan Sommers admits under my cross-examination that the prosecution does not know how or where the murder was committed or how the body was transported to the golf course.

The Hager nine iron is entered into evidence as the murder weapon but the photographs taken at the scene are missing. Is Harrington planning to put Tom Clement on the stand? Tom is standing in the back of the courtroom, which is illegal if he is to be called as a witness.

The state medical examiner delivers the physical evidence. I very carefully question him as to the cause of Mr. Leighton's death.

"Please state again for my clarification, the cause of death."

"Mr. William Leighton died of suffocation."

"Do you mean the original blow to his head did not kill him?"

"Yes. It may have rendered him unconscious, but no, it didn't kill him."

"Sir, I saw the body. The back of Mr. Leighton's head was smashed."

"Yes, that is correct, but those blows were administered after Mr. Leighton died."

"Can you tell the court if the golf club entered in evidence was the weapon used to crush his skull?"

"Mr. Leighton was struck by the golf club but from the remains I examined it was a single blow. I explained this to Mr. Harrington when I reported my findings."

I do not know what to do with my hands. I want to put them behind my back and cross my fingers. Harrington had not explained the full coroner's report to Dan Sommers.

"Sir, would you please state your findings for the court?"

"Some of what I'm about to say is guess work based on experience and as such isn't evidence. It was not in my formal report. Do you understand?"

I look up at Silas Morgan. He gives a slight nod in my direction."

"Sir, you are the state's expert and the prosecution's witness. In your learned opinion please help us discover the truth surrounding Mr. Leighton's death?"

Harrington does not object. He saw Judge Morgan agreed to allow the coroner's speculation to be entered in the court's record.

"Very well. William Leighton sustained a blow to the head which rendered him unconscious. A bag of some type was placed over his head and fastened around his neck above his shirt collar. There were faint ligature marks under his chin."

"Just a moment, sir. What are ligature marks?"

"In regards to Mr. Leighton the abrasions were across his Adam's apple. Such marks are a result of a constricting band being tighten around his neck. They were faint but present. It was impossible to discover anything from the smashed condition of his skull, other than he was dead when they occurred."

"Thank you for the calcification. How did you ascertain Mr. Leighton was dead when the final blows were administered?"

"His blood. When he died, he was lying of his left side. When the heart stops, the fluids in the body follow the law of gravity. His blood had started to pool on the left side of his body. The skull was crushed on the right side from which the blood had drained. I'm sorry that isn't a good explanation."

"I understand. Please finish with you personal conclusions."

"Mr. Leighton had to have been unconscious. There were no signs of a struggle on the body. He made no effort to remove the covering and suffocated for lack of air. From the small flakes of a rubber like material I found in the brain tissue, I surmised his head was still cover when the body was struck with a flat blunt object much like a hammer."

"Mr. Harrington, do you have any further questions of this witness?"

"No, your Honor."

Judge Morgan allows one half hour for lunch—to be served in the basement of the courthouse. He is keeping Harrington on a short leash; protocol demands that both the prosecutor and defense counsel honor his invitation. It is a silent box luncheon.

* * * * *

"Margery Endicott had a powerful motive to kill William Leighton. I call Callie Rogers to the stand.

Callie Rogers? What is he trying to pull? What would

she know about either Bill or Marcy? She was a kid when we graduated. I look at Marcy, but she shrugs her shoulders. The morning has taken its toll, I can see the bluish tinge under her eyes through her makeup. I put my hands on the table, ready to object before Callie reaches the stand.

Callie looks over her shoulder toward the audience. It is obvious she does not want to give testimony. Dragging her feet, she climbs into the witness box and swears on the Bible, snatching her hand away as if it burns. Harrington never mentioned her when we met on Friday.

She perches on the edge of the wooden chair and crosses her legs at the ankles, then studies her purse, refusing to look at anyone.

"Please state your name and occupation for the court."

Her answer is a stammer directed to the purse. "Callie Rogers—I'm a beautician."

"Miss Rogers, you must speak louder." Gilbert commands in his most pompous voice. Callie winces, then raises her head but keeps her eyes glued to the purse. She crosses her legs above her knees, and immediately, the leg begins to swing.

"Where were you on the night of Tuesday, May 22, 1955?"

"I. . . ."

I rise to my feet. "Your Honor, I must question the appropriateness of any events from fourteen years ago. What support can history lend to the current matter before the court?" I feel Marcy tense. From the corner of my eye I watch her grip the edge of the table.

"Mr. Harrington, will you please establish what bearing your witness has on the proceeding?"

"Yes, Your Honor." Gilbert's smile is smug. He has retaliated for the ban on publicity. "The witness for the prosecution will provide vital evidence as to Mrs. Endicott's motive for killing William Leighton Senior."

Gently reprimanding Harrington, Judge Morgan says, "Do not lead the jury to a conclusion before the fact. I will allow you to proceed with your questions. Mr. Fightmaster, I have noted your concern. Sit down."

"Miss Rogers, please describe the night in question, in your own words."

Harrington looks over toward our table, his smirk still intact. My bones read his silent message, "I've got you now."

"Jobi and. . . ."

"Miss Rogers, you must identify each person for the court record." Gilbert instructs her.

"Jobi Leighton. She was Jobi Andrews then. Jobi and I followed her brother, Phillip Andrews to a senior graduation party. I was driving my father's car. It was dark when we got to the ol' Hutchins' place. We walked down a dirt path to the cabin.

"It was silent. Eerie. You couldn't even hear a cricket. Jobi wanted to listen to what they were saying so we stopped in the woods at the edge of the clearing."

Callie looks up, searching the audience, her leg still moving. Her hands have the arm of the chair in a death grip. Her knuckles are white. She hesitates.

"Continue, Miss Rogers. What occurred when you reached the clearing?"

She takes a deep breath, and stares down at the purse. She refuses to look at the courtroom. "Marcy Lane was lying on the ground in a heap. Her skirt and crinolines were all pulled up around her waist. There were dirty spots, like grass stain on them. She wasn't wearing her underwear.

"Bill Leighton was kneeling beside her, his white shirt was also filthy and torn. Philip Andrews was standing over them holding a flashlight."

Marcy scribbles, "I didn't know they were there." on my legal pad, then clasps her hands together as if praying.

I am too stunned to even think. Marcy has let me come into this courtroom to defend her and did not tell me what happened the night we graduated.

Rule one: Lawyers do not cry when they have been betrayed by their client. I grit my teeth and follow her example: I pray that I can hang on through the afternoon.

Farral Masters looks up in shock from his Stenotype machine and loses his place in the testimony as Callie speaks the horrible words.

I have lost track of her story. I dare not look at Marcy. The malicious act has no connection to the people I have known my entire life. The room is silent. I can hear my heart pounding in my ears. No one moves as Callie condemns Marcy.

Callie blurts, "We thought she was dead. Everybody did. It wasn't until she appeared in that movie that we knew any different."

"That was later. I will repeat my question, "What happened when you entered the clearing? William Leighton was kneeling beside Miss Layne wearing a torn and dirty shirt. . . ."

"Objection, Your Honor, he is leading the witness to a conclusion." It is a feeble attempt to get my bearings.

"Objection, sustained. Rephrase the question, Mr. Harrington."

"Miss Rogers, in your own words, tell the court what happened in that clearing."

"Yes, Sir. Bill—William Leighton was kneeling beside Marcy Lane's body, his shirt was torn and dirty. They said she was dead. I started crying, I couldn't help it. Jobi Andrews was mad at me for being a baby.

"She told Bill and her brother to put Marcy's body in the root cellar because Tom Clement had told Elton Fightmaster the area was going to be bulldozed the next day. Jobi said no one would ever find her body buried under the new cabins.

"We were too scared to tell Miss Cynthia."

I remember Tom asking if I would go with him to watch the work. He wanted to write it up for the paper. His first real news story. I went out there that Saturday morning with him and he took a snapshot, for his memory book, of the old root cellar where my friends had played pirates. Something was odd about it; there was a heavy board pushed against the door. It was the same place Clayton Forrester had mentioned; Elroy and Lon had used it for their stash.

"Bill—William Leighton, told Philip Andrews to take us back to town. When we left, Bill was standing with his back to her body, looking off into the woods. Philip Andrews left the two of them in the dark. He used the flashlight to walk us back to where the cars were parked, then we went to Hamilton's Drug Store for a soda and waited for Bill. He came in a little later, wearing a clean shirt."

"Your witness, Counselor."

Callie is crying by the time I reach the bench. I hand her my handkerchief.

"Elton, I told the truth.

"Marcy, I'm so sorry; we thought you were dead." Her sobs shake the chair.

"I have no questions, Your Honor."

"Take the defendant to my chambers, Bailiff. We will take a ten minute recess." He bangs his gavel. The state policeman appears at Marcy's elbow and escorts her from the room by the side door. I help Callie down from the witness stand as Harrington darts up the aisle.

CHAPTER 20

I call Philip Andrews to the stand."

I crane my neck as Philip enters from the side door. He is sober. I can tell by the way he holds himself, but like Callie he drags his feet to prolong entering the witness box. His face is pinched and drawn; all of the physical good looks that he has always possessed have fled from his countenance.

"Mr. Andrews, when was the last time you spoke to William Leighton Senior?"

"A couple of days before he was killed."

"What did he say to you?"

"Bill said he was going to right a wrong that had existed for many years."

"Was he despondent?"

"Your Honor, I object to this line of questioning. I do not understand the relevance of the victim's mental state to his death."

"I tend to agree. Mr. Harrington, I will allow the witness to answer the previous question and then we will move on. Mr. Andrews, was Mr. Leighton despondant?"

"No, Your Honor. He seemed to be relieved of a burden."

"You may continue your questioning, Mr. Harrington."

"Mr. Andrews, what happened the night of May 22, 1955?"

"We graduated from high school." His voice has no inflection, but his bright-blue eyes follow Harrington's every move, like a cornered animal.

"Did you have a party after the ceremony?"

"We planned a celebration."

"Please tell the court what happened that night, in full. Use your own words, take your time, but do not leave anything out."

"I object, Your Honor. Mr. Harrington's instructions are confusing the witness."

"Sustained. Rephrase the question."

"Tell the court in your own words what happened the night you graduated from high school."

"A group of close friends planned to meet at the Old Hutchins place to have a few beers and celebrate."

"Just a minute, wasn't Elton Fightmaster a member of your special group?"

"Yes, he was."

"Why wasn't he invited to the party?"

Harrington is exhibiting a vicious streak. Everyone knows why I was not invited. He intends to humiliate me the same way he tried to hurt Marcy when she was arrested. Judge Morgan is frowning but does not interfere.

"Elton can't walk well enough to handle the terrain out there. We didn't want to hurt his pride, so no one told him."

"Thank you. I'm sorry for the interruption, but I needed to clarify the facts for the court records. Continue your story."

"Bill—William Leighton arrived before I did. A car shot past me as I turned into the lane and parked behind Bill's new Chevy. As I opened the door, I heard a scream, followed by a crash in the woods. It was very dark but I knew the path from playing there when I was little. I hurried down the path and when I arrived Bill was on his knees beside Marcy, slapping her in the face and saying her name over and over.

"I stumbled over a flashlight lying on the ground and picked it up. Then I turned it on to give Bill some light. Marcy didn't respond. Bill tried to listen for her heartbeat but he couldn't hear it. He said she was cold.

"At that point my sister and her friend, Callie Rogers, walked out of the woods. They were all dressed up like they were going to a dance."

Philip's hands start to shake on the arms of the chair. Is he going into delirium tremors right here in, the courtroom? I do not know how far his alcoholism has advanced.

"There is no excuse. We panicked. We—didn't know anything about dead people. We were scared. We listened to my sister." His voice is starting to shake. He pauses, takes a deep breath and continues in the same drone. "I took the girls back to town while Bill put Marcy in the root cellar."

"Mr. Andrews, the proscution finds this hard to believe. Mr. Leighton, you, and Elton Fightmaster were close friends. You've implied you never confided in Mr. Fightmaster."

Why is Harrington trying to implicate me in this dreadful story of the assault on Marcy? Does he plan to petition to have me dismissed from the defense? Is he that vindictive?

Philip places his hands on his knees to control the tremors but he stares almost blankly into Harrington's face. A spectral silence pervades the courtroom, all present are hanging on his every word.

"We never spoke to each other about what happened that night, much less Elton."

Harrington turns and walks back to his table picks up a sheet of paper, and twirls to face Philip.

"Did Bill Leighton rape Marcy Lane?"

"No! Bill loved her."

"Then who did?"

Philip hesitates, his voice shifts to a high pitch of agony, "My father."

"No!" Her scream echoes in my ears. Jobi Leighton flies around the table reaching for Marcy. I push her away as Philip jumps from the stand.

She is screaming, "My Daddy wouldn't touch that piece of trash. I'm his little love." She shoves the edge of the table into my chest, pinning me to my chair.

Philip makes a grab for her and catches a sleeve. She has nothing on but a thin nightgown. Marcy moves against me to dodge her claws.

Jobi is still screeching like a piece of chalk being dragged down a blackboard, "You killed my Bill. I saw you through the door. . . ."

There is a tiny flash of light as the sun hits her wedding rings. Breaking glass mingles with her shriek as Jobi Leighton falls backwards through the open window. Philip is left holding a piece of her sleeve in his hand; he opens his hand and it falls slowly to the floor.

Judge Morgan bangs his gavel and shouts orders. "Everyone return to their seats. Mr. Fightmaster, take your client to your office. Stay there until you are called. I'll hold anyone else who moves in contempt of court."

We leave by the side door, supporting each other.

CHAPTER 21

A s we make our way to the jail and my car, we look back towards the courthouse, Dan Sommers is stringing bright yellow tape from the banister railing to the parking meters on the street. A spot of pink shows above a white blanket. Philip is running down the front steps.

"Is she all right?"

"No way to tell. Dan Sommers or someone from the court will notify us, when they can. Did you hear her last words?"

'Elton, everyone in the courtroom heard her."

"Do you realize what has happened?"

"Yes, she said she saw me kill Bill, but I didn't. She is deranged. Even Harrington isn't dumb enough to accept what she said as valid."

Marcy does not understand Jobi's furious accusation has the strength of a deathbed confession. She is moving. She is saying the right words, but her face is blank. She has retreated into herself. Her body is standing behind a glass wall.

* * * * *

"Why did you keep this from me? How did you expect me to defend you if I did not know what happened?" I shout at her as I have never shouted at anyone in my life trying to break the barrier of my own fears.

"Philip identified his father as my attacker. Elton, I didn't remember who it was."

Her voice is dull, as flat as Philip's when he was testifying. There is a rote quality, to her words, as though she has memorized them. What she is saying finally penetrates the fog of my own fury. "You do not remember what happened?"

She shakes her head and her shoulders slump. "I knew I'd been assaulted, but who has always been blank." She pulls up her shoulders as anger flashes in her eyes.

I want to strike Phillip, hurt him for keeping this terrible secret from me.

"You should have told me."

"Why? You couldn't help."

"Marcy, Harrington intends to send you to electric-chair. I sat there, in that courtroom, with my hands tied, betrayed by my friends. Don't you understand? How did you get out of the root cellar?"

"Elroy and Lon. They were hiding a cache of Hank Sidmore's hootch and found me."

"Why didn't you tell me? Marcy, you let me go into that courtroom ignorant of the facts. How did you expect me to defend you?"

She is pacing from wall to wall, I try to follow her but my movements are torturous, so I compromise and lean against the edge of my desk. She whirls and glares at me across the room.

"You are repeating yourself. Elton, don't be an idiot. Did you see Cynthia Lane come in here and tell the truth?"

"Miss Cynthia? She has not come to town since you arrived. Does she know what happened the night you were. . . ."

"Raped, say it damn it, R A P E D, or is it still the woman's fault?"

I stand to my full height to refute her charges that I would consider assault the responsibility of the victim. She doesn't allow me to answer.

"That I do remember. I was conscious by then. *Of course* she knows. When they found me, they took me home. My mother. My precious mother slammed the door in our faces."

"Your mother?" The relationship hangs in the air between us, a point from which neither of us can return.

"Cynthia Lane is my mother," her words are sharp, ripping like the blades of a grinder, "not poor Mollie Burton. Would you like to hear that lovely story, too?"

Her torment is appalling, as her feet wear a path across the carpet. "She'd rather sit out there nursing her righteous hypocrisy, protecting her own mythological reputation. It's more important to her than I am. I'm nothing more than an accident of a passion she has spent a lifetime denying."

Her pain from all the years of being abandoned by the one person who should have protected her flood my office. She reads my thoughts with devastating accuracy.

"All these years, she let people believe I left town with a drummer. She never—not even once wrote me a letter Not even when I lost Kira Lynn and Jeremy Endicott was killed. I wrote her. She never answered.

"I went out there when I came home. She stood on the porch, with her arms crossed across her chest. I was begging, begging, but she closed the door in my face, leaving me standing there as she had that night.

"If you mutter one damn platitude about how times were different, or forgiveness, our friendship is over." She points to my father's portrait. "Can you ever forgive that bastard?" She dashes to the mantel and lifts the red bowl to hurl it at my father's picture.

"For God's sakes, Elton, wake up to the real world." Her anger matches mine and darts about the room, shooting dangerous sparks like the Wren when it burned.

"Elroy Harris and Lon Chambers found me in that root cellar. Lon is a nigger. Even in these enlightened times, the good old boys, your precious friends and neighbors," her voice rancorous with vitriol as it spits, "would hang him from the nearest tree if they knew I'd spent two weeks in his care."

I stumble toward her and grab the bowl just as it leaves her fingers, falling over her, knocking us both to the carpet. Her fists slam against me as I struggle to keep the bowl out of her hands and get to my feet.

Tears of anger and flustration stream down her face.

In retaliation, *I slap her*.

A loud hiccup erupts from her throat, as she stares at me while I put the bowl on the sofa and push myself upright. I am so ashamed, I cannot face the accusation in her eyes. I keep my back to her as I stand and walk to my desk, shaking from the mortification of my act.

"I deserved that for what I said about Lon." Holding her cheek, she gathers her coat and returns to her prison at Mrs. Carstairs; as she leaves, silence pervades the room.

I look at my father, whose painted eyes follow my every move in censure of my weakness. No real man would ever strike a woman, no matter what the provocation.

I take the bowl to the mantle and replace it; it rattles against the shelf from my trembling hands. Then I remove the painting, which leaves a pale space on the wall, reminding me it is time for new paint. I rehang the portrait and try to stare him down, but my soul refuses to accept his accusations of my worthlessness because my mother smiles benignly from her side.

No, Marcy, I've lived in his shadow for too long. He cannot hurt me any longer. My friends have replaced him in their evaluation of my unworthiness to share their lives.

What am I going to do to keep her safe from the condemnation of Jobi's words and my own violence? Philip has buried the memory of that night in alcohol, the terrible knowledge that his father assaulted his friend.

* * * * *

"Elton, Judge Morgan just released us. He asked me to tell you that court will reconvene on Wednesday morning. They forgot about us in the waiting room until just now."

"Thank you, Wilson."

"Where's Marcy?"

"Across the square where she is being held. I am going to have a drink—will you join me?"

Father Stanley and Rabbi Lehman remove their coats, tossing them over a chair. "The young woman was killed. Her neck was broken when she fell. A drink will be most welcome."

"Jobi?" We had forgotten Philip's sister. She was dead as we drove away to an afternoon of disclosures that ended in our confrontation of raw emotion. Hurting each other because we had no one else at whom to strike.

I start to rise, "Stay seated. I know where you keep the *Crown Royal.*"

Rabbi Lehman grins, "He has a nose for the good stuff

even when it is bottled and in a cabinet."

Monsignor Stanley pours a stiff shot into one of my mother's Waterford cordial glasses. "Now drink up and I will fix you another for sipping."

"Sir, are you trying to get me drunk?"

"Best medicine in the world for what ails the soul." I obey his instructions. I do not possess the fortitude to argue with a determined Catholic priest.

I pour the fine, difficult-to-obtain whiskey down my throat like water. Rather a waste of the best, but a gentle warm heat settles on my stomach.

He hands balloon glasses to my guests.

"The country club must have made those club sandwiches we had for lunch last week. I'm going to the Kricket to dig in the refrigerator for a decent dinner. Don't let him drive if you intend to keep pouring liquor into him. I'll have something ready in an hour." Wilson slips out the door, leaving me to the ministrations of two experts.

"The woman who fell, who was she?" Monsignor Stanley's soft-blue eyes are clouded for a woman he never knew.

"The wife of the deceased."

"The man Marcy is accused of killing?"

"Yes."

"We watched out the window as they were taking her away. Strange clothes to be wearing in a courtroom. What happened?" Ben Lehman's eyes wander around the room as if he expects Marcy to emerge from the shadows. Can he sense the violent accusations that have penetrated the walls of my office?

"She identified Marcy as Bill's killer just before she fell."

"That's absurd. Marcy didn't kill that man. She never

mentioned his name, not even in the most casual conversation, the entire time we've known her. But she talked of you often with deep affection. He was of no importance to her. There is no motive."

"Actually just the opposite, Bill Leighton is—was—the one man Marcy has loved all of her life. It was obvious when she came home, but they would never have overstepped the boundaries; too much time and distance stood between them."

"I see." He pauses and takes a small sip of his drink. "We can still help you with our testimony."

"Oh yes. Now even more so; everyone in that courtroom heard Jobi Leighton. Harrington tried to prove Marcy was assaulted by Bill the night we graduated."

"What?"

"Marcy remembered nothing about the cause of her illness, of that I can testify with assurance and not break the vows of the confessional."

Philip's ravaged face and Marcy's tormented one flash in the brown whirlpool in my glass. I raise my head, "She does now. She was reminded today, in court, just before Jobi Leighton died."

CHAPTER 22

I am eating a piece of toast. I answer the knocking on the front door so my head will stop pounding.

"Elton, you have a hangover!"

Phillip is standing on my porch making absurd comments. "I do?"

"I know the signs." He is not smiling.

"What are you doing here?"

"I need your help with Jobi's and Bill's estate. Neither of them had a will. The Gladen's have filed suit in Allerton County for custody of Little Bill. They are trying to have me declared unfit to administer his affairs."

"You had best come in. I am finishing breakfast."

"Thought you went to the Kricket every morning. I went there trying to find you. Tom Clement sent me here."

"Not up to getting out this morning." I awoke with the brace removed in my own bed. I do not want to consider what I told them in my drunken stupor. My secrets will remain secrets in their care. "You should be at Clark's."

"Something funny is going on. Dan Sommers won't

release her body for burial until after he finishes his investigation. What is there to investigate? She fell out the window. We all saw it happen."

"Philip, I have no idea. I have not seen Dan since I left the courtroom. I do have coffee and toast. Interested?"

"I could use some. But you with a hangover. How in the world did that happen?"

"After supper a priest and a rabbi helped me empty a fifth of *Crown Royal*. We may have started a second one, I do not remember."

"A priest and a rabbi did what?"

"Old army buddies of Elroy Harris and Lon Chambers. Ben Lehman is Marcy's agent and Monsignor Stanley housed her when she went to California. She was living in a convent for those three years when she was missing. It is too long a story to go into now. Eat and do not talk, the jam is on the table. Do you have a cigarette?"

He tosses me a fresh pack and gulps the cup of coffee, refilling his cup from the pot on the stove before he eats the toast.

* * * * *

"Coffee, is all I am going to offer you."

"Fine, it's all I want. I haven't taken a drink since you bailed me out of jail."

"Is that the truth? Where have you been?"

"In John Henry's tack room. He and Kathryn helped me get through the worst of the DT's. He made me exercise every horse on the place, even the brood mares that have never been broken except to a halter. I walked them for miles."

His fists are clinched in agony. A cigarette dangles from the edge of his lips, making him resemble a gangster from an old movie, but one with an angel's face.

"When Dan told me what Jobi was doing to Little Bill I was sick all over again. I knew I had to stop drinking. He is who matters now."

"Philip, before I can help you, I must know the full story of what happened the night we graduated. You testified under oath that your father assaulted Marcy. How did you know?"

"The flashlight. It was lying on the ground beside her. I picked it up and turned it on to give Bill some light."

"Yes, Callie Rogers said you were holding a flashlight when she and Jobi walked out of the woods. What is so important about a flashlight?"

"I—gave it to him for Christmas." He stubs out the cigarette and quickly lights another. "I've got to start smoking cigars, these don't last long enough. I'll go make another pot of coffee; we are going to need it since you've elected yourself to be my priest." He reaches in his pocket and pulls out his billfold.

"This is a retainer; now you are officially my attorney. Client confidentiality and all that it entails."

I stare at the hundred-dollar bill lying on the coffee table and look up at my father. I pick up the bill and toss it on my desk. I will have it framed for when I need to be reminded of the price of loyalty. It is the largest retainer I have ever received, and the most expensive.

* * * * *

"Look, Elton, this is hard to talk about. Being fools doesn't excuse our behavior, not what we did. You know there is—was—no love lost between Jobi and me, but she was my sister. I've thought about it most of the night.

Telling tales on your own family is rotten, especially when they are dead. That may be why the bastards of this world get away with it."

"Philip, you are rambling. What are you talking about? As I told Marcy, I cannot help when I am working in a vacuum." The hangover and rancid taste of too much coffee, combines with my resentment of being excluded from their confidence to make me argumentative.

"Little Bill first, while I work up the courage for the rest."

"You said you were being sued for custody of your nephew, because you are not reliable to manage his affairs."

"Elton, he doesn't have any affairs. That's what I'm trying to tell you. My father's will—left everything to me. It was made by your father, within a day or two after he got his draft notice. Jobi was born after he was in the army. He never believed Jobi was his daughter. I can still hear them fighting about it, he'd get drunk and start knocking my mother around. It couldn't have been—memories play tricks on you—but it seems like every night."

"Oh, dear. I never heard my parents quarrel." I am looking up at them from behind my father's desk. Philip is slouched on the Chesterfield.

"Clydsville is a small town, and everybody knows all the secrets, or they think they do. But the truth is behind closed doors, and some secrets last for generations.

"Anyway, the Gladens think there is money coming to Little Bill, but there isn't. Even the house belongs to me. Jobi kept Bill broke remodeling. He was never able to save a dime."

Philip is up and pacing. He stops by the window to finish his coffee, then returns to the kitchen for a refill. His hands are steady. I do not see the tremors I witnessed in court. I do not tell him to sit down though I wish he would. I have never known anyone coming off a fourteen-year binge. One night is all I can handle and I am not so sure of that.

"What I want you to do is draw up a trust for him. A college fund so the Gladens can't get their hands on it. I will sell the house and put the proceeds in the trust. Personally, I'd love to put a match to the damn thing. You can do that, can't you?"

"Do what? Torch the house or design a trust?

"Elton, you know what I mean."

"Of course, but in the interim, who will provide for him?"

"I'll pay through the bank. Beckworth can arrange it."

"Philip, how are you fixed financially? Can you afford it?"

"Residuals, the best kept secret in the insurance industry. My grandfather started the business in the twenties. When he died, my dad took over, then while he was in the army, mother ran the firm."

"Residuals from what source?"

"Whenever a policy is renewed, the agent who sold it,or the firm in our case gets a percentage of the premium. You know how people are here, they bought a policy years ago, and then each time they get a bill, they pay it. They seldom have any problems, so the policy just goes on and on. My mother was a whiz at selling small life insurance policies— that may have been one reason she and dad fought so much. She was a better salesman than he ever was. I can remember, when he came home, she wanted to keep working and he wouldn't stand for it. He didn't want her near the office."

"I see."

"Another habit of small towns: my daddy dealt with your daddy, so I will deal with you. I take after mother. I can and do sell insurance. I also take care of the policy holders. Now I'll have to work even harder with a child to support. I can't let anything happen to Bill's little boy. Next to Marcy, he loved him more than life. Bill only stayed with Jobi because of him. Odd, but Little Bill was the only child she was able to carry full term. She was pregnant when they married."

"He is living with your uncle. Give me his address."

"No, his grandparents have him. When I went over to see him last night, they wouldn't let me in the door. Mrs. Gladen called me a pervert."

"How did they find out?"

"I guess they got it out of him. You know how kids babble, or maybe he had a nightmare. Elton, I never harmed him, I swear. As far as I know, the funny stuff only started after Bill died.

"My sister was strange. When she was living with me. . .she got in bed with me. When I woke up, she was stroking me. I. . .had a. . .hard-on for my own sister! I had to keep the door locked or I'd wake up to her fondling me! She believed love was the physical act. She couldn't understand anything else."

He sinks down in a chair as if all the strength has drained out of him. I do not say a word. Philip's monologue has gone on and on, business mixed with terrible things that happened years ago. I am the only person he trusts, yet he had to make sure I am bound to silence.

"Elton, do you remember the night they died?"

" Your father called you at school about your mother's accident. Bill and I came home with you. What we found was horrible. Who could forget?"

"It wasn't an accident. He told me over the phone. Jobi pushed her through the banister."

"You did not tell us that."

"How could I? That my sister murdered my mother is not something I could tell even my best friends. Same as I couldn't tell Bill my father raped Marcy and left her for dead."

"But. . . ."

"That isn't the end of it. My father didn't commit suicide. He was executed."

"He was what?" I stand up, the room spinning before my eyes.

"Executed! Old man Clark found a .45-caliber bullet lodged in his spine—it had torn out his heart. My grandfather's shotgun blast at close range covered it up. My father didn't own a .45. The bullet was buried with him. Clark told me about it some years later before he retired."

"Did Jobi kill him too? Why did Clark cover it up?"

"No, I don't think so. Jobi adored him, she was always sitting in his lap with her arms around him. He'd give her anything she asked for. All she ever had to do was run to him if Mother even touched her. He'd take his belt to me if she claimed I did something to her; she was always saying, 'I'm going to tell my Daddy.'"

He is like a fountain. Once the pump is primed, the terrible truths keep spilling out. I cannot blame him now for the alcohol; it was the only way he had to prevent his mind from following Jobi into insanity.

"But you said he did not believe Jobi was his daughter. Their relationship seems strange if he. . . ."

"That's right; you just thought of it. It took me years and I lived in the house. My father—was having physical relations—with my sister. And. . .and my mother knew it. The nightgown Jobi was wearing when she fell belonged to my mother.

"You forget after Bill and Jobi married I lived with my Aunt Lena Sue before she died."

"The old Laurence bridal house, it is a fine place."

"It's a hell hole. I don't dare consider getting married, what if I have a daughter? My grandfather treated Aunt Sue the same way; it was in her diaries."

"My God, Philip. Have you been beating yourself to death over the actions of your father and grandfather?"

"Congratulations! I believe you finally are beginning to learn how to cuss. Took you long enough. Though how you managed with him," he points to the portrait of my father, "following your every move is beyond me. He's enough to make a priest and a rabbi take up drinking. Coffee is cold." He starts to the kitchen.

"Wait a minute. Under my father's rudimentary tutelage, I learned a vital precept, one he taught in reverse. *Never accept unearned guilt.* All this time, even in your cups, you have done the best you could under the circumstances. The acts were not yours, you cannot be guilty for something you did not do. I did not ask for infantile paralysis, it happened. . .an accident of fate.

"Lon Chambers taught me I could be like everyone else on a horse and he defeated my father, who wanted me to be a perfect specimen in his image. Think about it."

"In your roundabout way, I think you're saying: I punished myself by drinking because I couldn't punish them. I know their sins are not mine, but I have to live with the results.

"The future was beckoning until we listened to Jobi when we thought Marcy was dead, then everything went haywire. But Elton, I couldn't turn my own father in for murder after what we did."

"No more than you could turn in your sister on your

father's say-so. No one can blame you for protecting your family. You and Bill covered for her about other things over the years."

"How did you know Jobi stole things?"

"Philip, I do not have to remind you this is a small town. Word gets around. Bill Leighton stands accused of the bank fraud. Was he using the money to cover for Jobi?"

"No! Elton, I'll stake my life on it. Bill didn't touch one cent of the bank's money. Someone is setting him up as a fall guy. Bill was as honest as the day is long. I loaned him ten dollars till payday the afternoon before he was killed. He always paid me back immediately, before he paid any bills. The last thing he said to me was he was going to right a wrong that had existed for a long time."

"I thought Jobi killed him until Dan Sommers showed me it was impossible."

"I know. I did too. We know Marcy didn't, so who did kill Bill?"

"I have no idea. But why did Clark cover up your father's death?"

"His daughter was Dad's secretary. Clark said he had wanted to kill him himself and was glad that someone did."

"An execution is a father's rage?"

"Could have been, but Marcy's father died in the war. I don't know of anyone else."

"Make a fresh pot. I need a cup."

Clouds of cigarette smoke hover near the ceiling floating on the currents from the furnace. My office reeks, like Beckworth's at the bank. I get up and try to open a window.

"Here, I'll help you. It's cold out there."

Together we push the windows open.

CHAPTER 23

When Philip leaves, I examine the law books that once belong to my father. After much searching I find the volume I am looking for, in grayish-green buckram, the lettering faded from the spine: Franklin Kreml's, *The Evidence Handbook for Police.* Printed in 1947, it is the most recent volume I have for research.

I spend the evening and the next day combing its pages for enlightenment. The same conclusion keeps staring me in the face. There is not enough evidence to establish a "reasonable doubt" for Marcy. Not when the jury heard Jobi's words.

Wednesday morning WHAS and WLEX vans are parked on the square. The state trooper waves the reporters away from Marcy. I hear their shouted questions but ignore them. Harrington has spread the word and has been giving interviews. The television cameras block most of the curb in front of the stone steps.

As we start to cross the lobby after fighting our way through the swarm of reporters, Elroy and Lon fall in on each side of Marcy, barricading her state police escort with their grim visages. They are both wearing dark suits with colorful military bars pinned above the breast pocket. The cut is old fashioned, but they are constructed of choice worsted. British tailoring at its finest.

Elroy pulls her hand around his arm and puts his hand over hers. "Allow us, Marcy gal, to escort you into this humble den of iniquity."

The trooper does not try to stop the honor guard. I glance over my shoulder to where a priest, a rabbi—both in the same style suits and ribbons, and Wilson, are smiling as if the sun has been newly discovered. The lone officer walks behind them as Marcy's tinkling laugh resounds to something Elroy whispers in her ear as we climb the worn steps. The flash from Tom Clements' single-lens reflex blinds me for a moment.

I can picture four young GI's in London with combat pay burning a hole in their pockets, being fitted for those suits before they are shipped home. Over twenty years later, they still fit.

People part to let us pass. Reverend Haskins stands stiffly to the side as we come to the open doors of the courtroom. He clutches a worn Bible and raises his left hand as if to give a benediction. In the stillness of the waiting crowd his voice seems to bellow.

"The wages of sin is death."

"Shucks Preacher, if the devil don't pay no better than that. I won't work for 'em."

Marcy's hand closes on his arm, and I hear some strong snickers behind us. Reverend Haskins stomps away with both hands gripping the Bible, muttering about idolaters defacing God's temple. A crocheted-cross bookmark flutters to the floor. It is immediately covered by a large mud-covered

Red Wing boot, belonging to whom I am not sure.

Lon retreats to the balcony while Monsignor Stanley and Rabbi Lehman follow Elroy and Marcy into the courtroom. I stand aside with Wilson and let them precede us. The clergy execute a perfect four-point turn and come back up the aisle, holding their right-hands high with their fingers spread in Churchill's sign for victory.

Wilson hands me a note as they pass.

> When it is your turn, call Elroy to the stand.
> He holds all the Aces. We will be on the
> back row, you won't need us. JBS

* * * * *

Judge Morgan waves his hand to silence Gilbert Harrington when Philip assumes his seat on the witness stand. Philip looks like my friend from high school. His eyes are clear as he hesitantly smiles at Marcy. He must make his own peace with her.

"Mr. Andrews, in view of the tragic circumstances of Monday's proceedings, please accept the court's condolences."

"Thank you, Your Honor."

"Do you have anything to add to your previous testimony?"

"No, Sir. I told the truth on Monday."

"Since you have nothing further to add, you are excused."

"I object, Your Honor. I have more questions of the witness."

"Objection, denied." He bangs his gavel. "Mr. Fightmaster, the court is ready for the defense to present its case. Call your first witness."

I rise to my feet and find I am not even nervous, though I have no idea what will transpire. Serene is the mood of these men who love Marcy and have supported her through the years. Elroy must be holding more than aces, he must have a royal heart flush. Even Marcy is relaxed in their presence. Her posture reflects none of the tension I sensed in her on Monday.

"Your Honor, I call Mr. Elroy Mason Harris to the stand."

"I object, Your Honor. Mr. Harris is not listed on the defense docket."

"Sir, when the trial began, Mr. Harris was snow-bound in upper Minnesota, hence unable to appear for the defense."

"I see. Objection, denied. Proceed." It is clear that Judge Morgan is furious with Harrington for alerting the press and grandstanding before the television cameras, though technically the gag-order is no longer in effect.

After the swearing-in, Elroy elegantly seats himself, turns his back to Judge Morgan, looks at Gilbert Harrington with contempt, and crosses his eyes.

I fight to keep from laughing out loud. I have no idea how to question him so I use the same ploy Harrington used with Callie and Philip. "Mr. Harris, please tell the court, in your own words, what happened the evening of December 10, 1968."

"I went fishin'." He winks at me.

Good heavens, Elroy. Marcy's freedom is at stake. Harrington is not the person to antagonize. What are you trying to do?

"Were you alone?"

"No, Sir. Lon Chambers was with me and. . . ."

"Your Honor, Chambers is not listed on the docket nor is he in court."

Before Judge Morgan can admonish Harrington for interrupting the witness; Elroy's eyes blaze in fury.

"He is too in court. He's up in the balcony, which is the only place he can look down the likes of you."

Judge Morgan bangs his gavel. "Mr. Masters, strike those last statements from the record beginning with Mr. Harrington's interruption. You sir, will allow Mr. Fightmaster his privilege of interviewing his own witness. If you repeat this performance, we will adjourn to my chambers."

"Mr. Harris, who else was with you?"

"Elton, Marcy was with us. Dan Sommers knows it."

"Sheriff Sommers! How did he know Marcy was with you?"

"He helped us put the boat in the water."

"Where did you put the boat in the water?"

"At the headwaters of Grasshopper Creek before it runs into the lake. Best ramp on the lake."

I am too excited to be sensible. That boat ramp is fifteen miles from town, and Dan Sommers was in town when I got to the square the night of the fire. Marcy did not say a word. Suddenly, I understand; she was protecting them.

The rules of evidence. Time. Time is important. I must establish the time.

"Mr. Harris, what time did this take place?"

"You'd best check with the Sheriff to be sure, but I'd say around eleven. He'd been out there checking on those summer homes because someone had reported a prowler. Said he was heading back to town when he pushed us off."

"Can the Sheriff identify Marcy?"

"Don't know. She was wrapped up in an my old Pea jacket over a May West and wearin' a baseball cap."

"How long were you out fishing?"

"About an hour or so. The wind go up and it was cold.

Besides the fish weren't bitin'. Loaded out the boat, took it back to the barn and unhooked the trailer."

"You put the boat in a barn? Where?"

"Above our place."

Their place is near where Lost Man Creek empties into the river. Ten miles out Hard Ridge Road.

"Marcy picked up her car and followed us back to town; Lon was drivin'. I don't see too well at night, anymore. We watched the glow in the sky comin' up 1020. Knew somethin' big was on fire. She almost rammed the back of Lon's truck when he ducked in the parkin' lot of the Kricket. Got Wilson up and they started makin' coffee and sandwiches. We took off to town. She rode in with him holdin' the last load of sandwiches."

"Your witness, Mr. Harrington."

"Mr. Harris, you have told this court Mrs. Endicott was out on the lake with you and Chambers—fishing. Why would she keep company with two disreputable moonshiners?"

"She likes to fish. We taught her when she was a pup."

Harrington shakes his head, knowing Elroy will not say anything he can disprove. "No further questions, Your Honor."

"Mr. Fightmaster, there is no need to call the Sheriff to the stand. He has been nodding his head the entire time Mr. Harris was telling his story. Mr. Harrington?"

"The charges are withdrawn, Your Honor."

"Jury is excused. Case dismissed." Marcy is in Elroy's arms as the gavel slams. He holds her tight. Then he steps back as Lon approaches, and hands her to him.

Tears are running down their faces. "Now Marcy gal, you know it isn't seemingly to make displays in public."

CHAPTER 24

I have a good script on my desk, perfect for you. Are you sure you won't go back with us?"

"Ben, I've had enough drama this last week to last me a lifetime."

"What he is trying to say, Marcy, is we miss you."

"Thank you, Father Bryan. Last night I spent the first night in over a week at my new house, it was heaven."

"Marcy gal, we went by to check on it for you. Now, now don't go gettin' up a head of steam. Just turned up the heat and looked around."

"You told us you were painting, but why did you paint the windows pink?"

"Lon, that isn't paint, its Glass Wax. It was a warm day and I was cleaning windows when I got arrested."

Wilson indicates his broad windows, "I use Windex, easier on the lettering."

"Opal uses vinegar."

"Do you expect me to report in the *Banner* that the major discussion after the trial of the century by the participants was the cleaning of windows?"

"Why not? It's the truth."

"No one will believe it."

Phillip looks at me and winks; we both have Mrs. Tucker do our windows. From the odor, I would say she uses ammonia.

The Kricket is packed this morning. Monsignor Stanley and Ben Lehman are flying back to California this afternoon. Our family breakfasts have grown but they have a wonderful feeling. Philip was hesitant to intrude, but Marcy welcomed him with open arms. Mese has taken Sunny home for a nap and Tal got on the bus a few minutes ago. We linger, drinking coffee.

Beckworth and Harrington come in. Gilbert heads to their back table but Beckworth comes over. "Elton, I'm sorry I had to duck out of the witness room but the state examiner arrived and I had to go to the bank."

"No need to apologize. I did not even know you left, and, as it turned out, your testimony was not necessary."

"He doesn't mean yesterday, Elton. He left on Monday, just before the young woman died."

"Bill Leighton's death has ruined the bank. I don't know if I'll ever get the affairs cleared with the mess. . . ."

"Cadel, if you are implying Bill took money from the bank, *don't*. Bill would never have. . . ." I can hear Philip grinding his teeth.

"Maybe not; maybe he was covering for your sister. Too late now; the damage is done and the money is gone."

Philip's blue eyes turn as hard as a drill-bit, "Listen carefully Beckworth, because I'm only going to say this one time. I personally covered Jobi's pilfering. Every merchant in town knew to come to me. Jobi picked up things, always did. She even stole the radio she gave me for graduation, from Harry Bidwell's father-in-law. My dad took care of it.

"Jobi was my sister and Bill Leighton was one of my best friends. You keep your nasty speculation to yourself. I say if you want to find where the money went, find the person who killed Bill."

Beckworth frowns but does not comment. He crosses the room to join Harrington, who is still simmering after seeing his landmark case slide through his fingers.

"Philip. . . ."

"Sorry Elton, that sanctimonious jackass gets my dander going. Jobi and Bill deserve peace and absolution, not his sly innuendos."

Elroy places his hand on Philip's arm. "Enough. We'll deal with leftovers later. This is a party and I have a Clem story for the occasion.

"Bryan was visitin' Keenland on an April afternoon. Clem had never seen a man wanderin' around wearin' a long black dress with a white collar. He was fascinated by this weird person and watched him move through the benches below the stands where you can sit right behind the fence and watch the races.

"The horses were comin' up the concourse for the second race. Bryan slipped under the red velvet ropes and patted the head of a grey horse. Clem then followed him to the betting windows. Clem saw him put real money on the horse to win.

"Clem checked his pockets. He didn't have much except his bus money home, but he put it on the same horse. It was a long shot: 34 to 1 odds.

"Yessirreebob; the horse won.

"Clem pocketed his winnin's and stuck close all

afternoon. Each time Bryan touched a horse on the face it was a long shot, but it won. Clem was excited; he'd never had so much money in his life.

"He followed Bryan into the food arena and ordered a beer and a foot-long chilli dog just like the strange man.

"He overheard the bartender ask Bryan, 'Havin' a good afternoon, Father?'

"'Yes, my son. Just lovely.'

"Clem now understood. The man's son worked at the race course and was slippin' him tips.

"The last race of the day came up and the bartender's father slipped under the ropes and patted a bay gelding on the head, then he reached down and patted each hoof going all around the horse. Clem raced back to the bettin' windows pullin' all of his winin's from his pockets. He bet everythin' on the race and ran back to the fence.

"The horse came in dead last. Clem turned dejectedly from the fence. The strange man was calmly sittin' on a bench finishin' a beer.

"What happened? All day long when you patted a horse on the head, it won."

"That's the trouble with you Protestants! You can't tell the difference between a blessing and the Last Rites."

"May the light shine on your wickedness, Elroy. I'll light a few candles for you when I get home. You're going to need them."

"Better do a few black candles in the basement to hit all the bases."

"Humph! Marcy gal, will you take us to the airport? Wilson's car is too cramped."

I start to get up but Dan Sommers' hand closes on my arm. "Elton, stick around after everyone leaves. You too,

Philip. Tom, you'd just as well stay put. Have some more toast so it's not obvious." He shoves the plate and the jam pot toward us.

"Fine with me, I wanted to ask you about Jobi. Need to arrange her funeral." Philip spreads a slice thick with butter and heaps on the blackberry jam, enough to make a cake.

"Opal has wasted more berries trying to make jelly. She just can't do it. But she makes fine jam. Wilson got it from her."

"Jobi is why I need to ask you some questions. Don't want to do it in the office, too many Nosey-Parkers." Dan's eyes are on Harrington and Beckworth at the counter paying their bills. Both men ignore the bright yellow pig. They nod toward our table as they leave.

"I want each of you to tell me what you saw when Jobi went out the window. Tom, you take notes. I can't listen and write at the same time."

The back door slams. Marcy comes over, pulls out a chair and sits down beside me.

"I thought you were driving to Capital City."

"Spend two hours with those four, telling stories to see who can top whom. No way! Besides, my presence would cramp their style. Lon is driving, so my car and its passengers will be safe."

"Strange combination of friends."

"Not really. The religious vocations came later. Father Bryan was the navigator and Ben the tail-gunner on the same bomber. Elroy was the chief mechanic and Lon—I guess he was a cook. Whatever he did, he won their deep respect; to them he is their equal, maybe more, as if in the war he outranked them or something. Haven't you noticed how they defer to him?"

"Now that you mention it, yes. Maybe it is natural. He

has an inherent dignity that is hard to describe; my father could not face him down."

"Too bad it's February and the tracks are closed. Father Bryan loves the races. His family has their own box at Santa Anita."

"Now I know where I saw them! They spent an afternoon at John Henry's while I was exercising some mares. Overheard the priest doing some serious talking about buying one of the yearlings. Too fogged to think much. . . ."

Marcy's tinkling bells ring, "If he found one he likes, his family will buy it and he'll practically live in its stall, training it. Horses are his besetting sin."

"He isn't bad with *Crown Royal*."

"Elton, you didn't try to drink with them?"

"He did and lost. I saw him the next morning."

"You, poor dear, I should have warned you."

"Marcy, I need to talk to Elton and Philip. You shouldn't be here."

"Sheriff, I was present in that courtroom. I saw what happened. I'm the person she accused of killing Bill before she fell. We know I didn't kill him, so I have every right to be here." Her words are stiff, brooking no nonsense.

"Yes, Ma'am."

We each tell Dan what we saw. The stories are different in some details but essentially the same. We were looking from different angles. "Dan, why are you so concerned about the accident?"

"I talked to Judge Morgan first. He was sitting higher on his bench and had a full view of the room. He saw Jobi come in the double doors and start walking down the aisle as if in trance. When Philip named his father as Marcy's assailant she started screaming and ran the final few feet.

162

Then things started happening. He saw her lunge for Marcy, but by then people were on their feet rushing to the front."

Dan pulls a piece of wood from his vest pocket. It is broken and smashed.

"This is part of the window frame. It was entangled in her hair."

"What?"

"Yes, Philip. I know those windows are old and dry-rotted. The furnace was on-the-blink, and the window was half-open to cool the place off. Yet Jobi hit that window hard enough to shatter both the frame and the glass. There wasn't enough space between the table and the window for her to take a running jump backwards. It doesn't make sense. That's what has been bothering me.

"I have talked to everyone who was seated behind you. They tell the same story you did. I was hoping some of you saw something different."

"Dan, are you saying you think Jobi was pushed through that window?"

"Yes, Elton. I am. Something isn't right, but so far the only discrepancy I have is you saying you saw a tiny flash of light. How did you say it 'like the sun striking her engagement ring?'"

"That's correct. It was tiny but brilliant, and only for an instant."

"She wasn't wearing any rings."

"Oh dear. . . ."

"Dan, she must have seen Bill's killer, as she was trying to scratch my face."

"How do you figure that? You said you leaned against Elton to get away from her."

Marcy tilts her head and changes direction.

"She couldn't have seen me through the door of my room. I wasn't there and it was locked. I still have the key in my bag."

She opens her purse and starts digging for the old key. "It isn't here. I thought sure I dropped in my bag as I started down the hall."

"You only used one key for both doors."

"No, the one with my stuff was locked from the inside. Why? That's how your sister got into my things! I must have dropped the key to my bedroom. She found it in the hall."

Philip shakes his head and looks at Marcy. "Jobi took things. She may have stolen one from the desk; most of those old keys would have opened any door in the Wren. How she got in isn't important now.

"I know she started the fire, but where did she get the gas? Her car was at home, she was walking. She had on riding boots. Oh God, those were yours. Bill's can is still in the garage by his lawn mower. I saw it there the other day."

"Does anyone know anything about Jobi's movements that night, before I found her in the woods?" Tom is flipping through his notes.

"We had to break down the doors to your rooms. Both were locked the night of the fire. I glanced in Marcy's room before we cleared the floor the night of the fire, Dan. Her bed had not been turned down. Jobi could not have seen Marcy through a door.

"Remember, she said, 'You killed Bill. I saw you through the door.' Right before she fell. She was screaming at someone."

"Wilson, stop leaning on the counter and get me some white paper."

"Here, Marcy. Why do you want paper?"

"For blocking a story board. Thanks.

" Come on, we're going to the courthouse."

"What for?"

"Philip, your sister was murdered. It's a crime scene."

"So?"

"Use your head for something other than a siphon." Marcy has not completely forgiven Philip's rough riding his horse to exhaustion.

"Don't you know anything about how movies are made?" He shakes his head, but does not lower his eyes.

"It's all plotted, each actor has a mark on the floor, so the camera can catch their faces.

"The person who pushed Jobi through that window has to be someone who was in the courtroom, near the window."

* * * * *

Marcy is sitting at the judge's bench drawing a diagram of the room. "Now look." She jumps down.

"When you see a movie, you watch people move around, talk, do whatever. Every move each actor makes is mapped out on a story board—diagramed so they know their places. In a scene they must stay in the cameraman's full view. It takes dozens of sheets if a scene is active with a number of actors. No one can stay still except for a few moments.

"Now what we are going to do is map what happened when Jobi fell. Do you follow me?"

We nod like school children.

"The x's mark the position of each person. The witnesses came in through the door over there by the jury box.

"Dan, where does that door by the window go?"

"Marcy, that's the door to the fire-escape. I went out that way after Jobi fell."

We worked for an hour or more. Marcy's diagrams have everyone placed at different points during the fracas. Dan supplied the names of the spectators sitting in the pew behind us. Joan Butcher, Nancy Sharp, and Eloise Cutter were sitting directly behind us. Louise and Harry Bidwell were next to them, then Thelma and Norman Perkins with Vern Osborne on the end by the fire exit.

When Jobi pushed the table against me and started for Marcy, the ladies shrank back in their seats and started screaming.

Thelma Perkins said, "She's got on her night gown!"

I did not remember her exclamation until Dan read it from his notes. Louise Bidwell reached over trying to quiet the screaming and saw Philip jump from the stand.

When he reached Jobi, he managed to catch her left sleeve trying to pull her away from Marcy. Everyone was on their feet, Harry had told Dan he was reaching for Jobi when she started to fall backwards. Vern Osborne admitted to the Sheriff he tripped over Thelma's purse and fell to his knees.

I was pinned by the table with Marcy against my arm trying to dodge Jobi's hands. I heard the glass break, saw the flash of light but did not hear the wood of the frame splinter. I heard Jobi's last words, her scream and then I saw Philip holding part of a pink sleeve.

I watch Marcy look at her drawings, go to the table, sit in the chair and lean to the right. Then she walks to the fire-door and tries to open it.

"It's locked. Dan, you said you went down the outside stairs after she fell. Did you unlock it?"

"No, it was open a crack when I reached it. I have a

master key that opens all the doors. Let me open it for you and I'll show you how it stood."

Marcy steps out on the iron steps. "Dan, where does this ladder go?"

"To the roof."

Philip has been hanging back trying not to look toward the boarded window. His face is drained of color, leaving a tired old man to stare from shrouded blue eyes.

"There are two sets of stairs, and a catwalk around the dome. The other one is on the far side of the building. Bill and I climbed up there one time and dropped water balloons on people going in the courthouse." His words are slow, a painful memory of a friendship destroyed.

"Dan, did you see anyone on the stairs?"

"No, I was looking down, trying to watch my steps. Those old iron steps are different from normal risers."

Philip looks up, his finger pointing to the dome. "If the bastard went up the ladder to the roof and you were looking down, he could have been right above you and you wouldn't have seen him."

"Where is the other fire-door?"

"In a little alcove between a conference room and the judge's office."

Philip is still looking up, "Say he went out the far fire-door, crossed the roof and entered through this door. It's an illegal fire-door, it opens to the inside. All the killer had to do was stand behind the door, grab Jobi by the shoulder and fling her backwards. It would have taken a strong man; when she was in that state, she was hard to hold."

He walks through the door and stands on the fire escape. "I can see the table from here and the front of the courtroom." He pulls the door three-fourths of the way closed.

"Elton, I can see you. Move over to where Jobi started

for Marcy. Good. Can you see me?"

"Yes!"

"Then maybe Vern didn't fall over the purse but was tripped on purpose. The killer struck Jobi, knocking her over Vern towards the window. Then backed out the door going up the ladder to the roof as we rushed to the window."

"Tom, did you get everything down? Philip, that is a good idea but it has a few holes and too many maybes. Marcy, let me have those papers.

"It wasn't an accident when Jobi died. I thought I was going nuts."

He runs the three fingers on his left hand through his straw-colored hair. A gesture of pure relief.

"Your storyboards have been a great help. We know how she was killed and we know how the killer got away but we don't know who. It's like he was invisible."

Bill was right. Philip is almost a skeleton. His suit hangs in folds from his shoulders. He flops down on a bench.

"I thought I'd killed her. She fell when I was the only one who had a hand on her. I remember seeing Vern get up from the floor. I thought she knocked him down."

I walk over to him and put my hand on his shoulder. "There was nothing you could have done to prevent her death." Marcy sinks down beside him.

He looks up at me, his eyes sad and dim, "Unearned guilt?"

"Exactly."

Tom is perched on the edge of the table that pinned me against the ladies's legs. He is flipping back though his notes, "A minor detail. Dan, you said the fire-door was ajar. Was the other fire-door unlocked?"

"Yes. They must be unlocked before a trial begins in case of fire. I think the clerk-of-courts does it." He takes out his notebook and jots a few words. "I'll have to ask Farral Masters."

"It would have been easy for the killer to cross the roof and come down the far ladder while all was confusion on this side of building. He could come in, then go down the main stairs, and no one is the wiser."

"In a nutshell, Elton. For now, keep this exploration of the crime scene under your hats. I'm serious, I don't want Harrington crowding me.

"Elton, you and Philip go out the side door, go over to Maud Tosh's office. Find something about Bill's estate to keep her busy.

"Marcy, after they leave, wait a few minutes then slip out. Make sure no one is in the hall, go down the stairs, and over to the jail. If anyone stops you to gossip, tell them you're looking for me, that you forgot something at the jail."

"You mean, like my rubber gloves?"

He laughs; we all do, but Philip looks bewildered.

"I will tell you later. You want Maud to check for any property Bill may have owned."

"Tom, we will go out together but you come back with your camera. Take a picture of the window and put something in the paper. Suggest the windows and frames be replaced. That should get everyone stewing about higher taxes to pay for the repairs."

"I was planning to do it anyway. Those old windows are dangerous; they need grills on the outside. Now that Philip has pointed out those illegal doors, I will wager every door in the place swings the wrong way. The old diehards will threaten to cancel their subscriptions when I propose spending that much money. But why all the subterfuge?"

"I'm new at this job, feeling my way. Don't you realize what will happen when Harrington finds out we have a murderer who has killed two people? He was at the jail last evening raising hell about our investigation of Bill's death. He's mad because he lost his big show and everyone, including Judge Morgan, prevented him from making a federal case out of it."

"Do not worry about his hot air. You were elected because you are the best man for the position. From my viewpoint you are doing an excellent job."

"When I wanted to hide something from Jobi, I'd put it where she could see it; if I didn't, she'd take it. When she got in my room, she'd go through every drawer. That's what happened. She was killed, in plain sight."

CHAPTER 25

Elton, it's all over town."

This morning his bowtie is bilious. It is not khaki, but near spilled mustard in mud. The mustache has been trimmed to a fine line like William Powell's. It looks better than his earlier soup strainer.

"What is?"

"Nancy Sharp called Betty last night. Her new story is that Bill Leighton was paying Marci Layne blackmail to keep quiet about the rape—with the money he stole from the bank. That's why, according to Nancy, Marcy is so rich."

"Oh, dear. That is absurd."

"Granted, but the gossip mongers won't let it rest. The truth is not as fascinating as the illusion. Marcy is being tried all over again, and this time she can't face her accusers."

"What did Betty say?"

"You know her; she let Nancy ramble and then said, 'Thank you,' and hung up vexed worse than a cat with its paw in a mousetrap. She burned the mashed potatoes."

"In high school they were friends. You should have

heard them the day Marcy visited court with me. Their comments were vicious and they intended for Marcy to hear them. Why do they hate her so much?"

"I can tell you."

Wilson is standing by the table with our plates, there are only five. He puts them down and fills the coffee pot before he sits down.

He takes a sip of coffee. "Marcy has five things they can't tolerate: wealth, friends, beauty, talent and fame. I'm thinking of posting her picture outside the door so those cats won't come in. It was everything I could do not to dump their meals in their laps when they were in here the other day. They act like they are doing me a favor by eating here."

Philip and Dan arrive while I am thinking about Wilson's evaluation. I am afraid he is correct. He has a way of condensing the truth to a few words. Considering how other women hate her it is not surprising that all her friends are male.

"Where is everybody?" Dan asks as he hangs his coat and hat on the Victorian stand by the door.

"Elroy and Lon had a late night delivery. Marcy has taken Sunny, Tal and Mese to Cincinnati. I fixed them a picnic breakfast to eat on the way. Your breakfast is getting cold." He looks at the clock, "You're late."

"Wilson, you forgot the biscuits and jam."

* * * * *

Spring passed. We always have one, but for the life of me I cannot remember it. It was cold and damp up into June. Then the heat of summer generated mold on all the porch furniture and window sills. I have dusted the roses in Mother's garden a dozen times, but blackspot is turning the leaves yellow, and I am left with spindly, thorned canes.

The front screen door slams. "What are you working on? We were going riding."

"A trust for Bill Jr., I am setting it up for Philip."

"He's going to meet us at John Henry's, so it doesn't have to be completed today. After the rain last night it's fairly cool this morning. Great for a ride."

"Be with you in a moment. I had an idea I want to discuss with Philip. I am borrowing from your will."

"Oh!"

"Ready." I am dressed for riding but hiding the jodhpurs and boots behind the desk. Just have to change my jacket. "We will talk as we ride."

"Elton, he seems sober when he is with me. Is he?"

"Marcy, he is trying very hard, but I know this business of Bill and Jobi's unresolved murders is preying on his mind. So far so-good is all I can say."

Marcy and Philip are alike in many ways; they are much too thin but eat as if it was their last bite. The ghosts that pursue them will never go away. We all have phantoms from the past to some extent, but not like my two best friends.

I go riding with them once, sometimes twice a week, but John Henry tells me they are out for hours nearly every day. Marcy tends to disappear for a few days at a time; once she was gone for over a week.

Philip, on the other hand, has taken on the chore of serving as an exercise boy for John Henry, which means being there at four in the morning before he joins us for breakfast at six-fifteen. John Henry says he should pay him a salary like the other stable hands, but he does not want to get cold-cocked.

* * * * *

"Take that ugly picture down. Hide it in the attic if you must keep it."

"He was my father. This was his office."

"So. Do you intend to spend your life in his museum?"

I enjoy teasing Marcy. I have asked Isaiah Young to do a portrait of her. He was hesitant because painting individuals is not his forte, but agreed to do it if I did not mind waiting as he has a full load with his studies and teaching fellowship. He decided to render her as he had known her while they were working on her house. I have a rough sketch in my desk. When it is finished, I will surprise her with the portrait hanging beside my mother. The attic is a good place for my father.

"You had a lifetime of his telling you how much smarter he was than you."

"No, I do not believe he ever compared my intelligence to his."

She ignores me and bends her head to the left as if considering a profound statement.

"I had six years of what I know now was verbal abuse. Jeremy was good at kicking you where you live. To him I was a hick from the sticks who just barely finished high school."

"Why did you marry him if he was contemptuous of your background?"

"That was later. I never dated when I first went to California, and when I did they weren't real dates. The studio arranged for me to be seen with up-and-coming young actors. You have no idea, what a real jerk is until you've had to fend off some of those characters. I got so I wouldn't go unless Ben or Father Bryan waited in the background to take me home."

"I read some of those stories and thought it was your new life."

I cannot admit to her that I had collected every word. I have been doing a small house cleaning. I am keeping the lovely pictures in a scrapbook, but all the stories are going in the trash, where they belong.

I get up from behind my father's desk and take a chair facing the fireplace. She turns on the Chesterfield to face me, her back to my father's prying eyes.

"Elton, it was part of fantasy-land. The fans wouldn't be begging for more stories of Marci Layne at home, alone, reading a book, which is why I fell so hard for Jeremy Douglas Endicott III. He was a Harvard graduate who had a fabulous career and inherited money.

"When I first met him, I was deluged with flowers and courtesies. I'd never known anyone who was truly sophisticated. He could tell just by listening to chamber music which was a viola solo or a cello, while I'd never seen those string instruments.

"He couldn't do enough for me. The best restaurants, gala premieres, balcony box seats at the opera, he always had tickets to something grand and glamorous. The trouble started with little things, like how I dressed when at home or what I read for pleasure or wanted to do for fun and relaxation. I didn't pay much attention at first. I was trying too hard to please him and work at the same time.

"The one thing he could never find fault with was my riding. It was obvious I was the better equestrian. I never told him about Elroy, Lon and John Henry's father's horses. Our precious summers were too sacred to share. Even with the husband I thought I loved."

She jumps up and paces the room, fingering the papers lying on the table under the window. She is very nervous and driven by a force I do not understand. Marcy is hurting from all that has taken place since she returned home, yet she refuses comfort.

"He hated my riding ability, while he was club-fisted and would saw the horse's mouth till it bled. Once I tried to tell him how to hold the reins; it was a bad scene.

"Kari Lynn is the only reason our marriage lasted as long as it did. After she was born, he was jealous of both her and my work. He was devastated when I didn't win the Oscar and blamed Ben for putting me in the wrong part.

"He only hit me one time. No one had ever hit me before; it was such a shock. I left and sued for a divorce. To him I was incompetent to care for his daughter. He took our daughter and hid her. I think he intended to blackmail me into dropping the divorce proceedings, not to protect Kira from her own mother. I have no idea what crazy motive was in his mind."

She stubs out the cigarette and pulls a lock of her hair over her shoulder, twirling it around her fingers. My own hands itch to reach out to those shimmering strands of silk, but I can see the firm glass wall between us. I am allowed to see through but can never pass through the barrier. To Marcy, I will never be anything but a dear friend.

"She wasn't in the car when it was uncovered after the avalanche, nor were her things. He was dead, without a trace of her.

"In many ways Jeremy Endicott was not a bad man. He worshiped Kira Lynn. That sounds like a contradiction but it's true. Love and jealousy are two sides of the same coin. She has my hair and eyes, but now she is out there somewhere and I can't find her."

She reaches for another cigarette from the box on the coffee table and I light it for her.

"Ben has helped me. For two years we've had teams of detectives searching for her, but nothing has ever turned up—not one clue. Ben sent me a few pictures of her and that is all I have of my daughter. I pray every night that she is safe.

"He didn't plan on dying. He let his anger with me rule his decisions. He never dreamed I would leave him. It was strange, but he imagined I was the person I portrayed in the movies. When I look back, even that explanation doesn't make sense. He knew I was reared on a farm. I've never understood how anyone who knows anything about life wouldn't realize the strength that is bred into farm children. Survival is so elemental, you live with it every day of your childhood. He loved the star with a fierce obsession but never knew me as a person.

"Elton, I've rambled on and I appreciate your listening. It isn't the sophisticated, glamorous world the public is led to expect."

"I knew part of it; Ben Lehman told me about your life the night we were drinking."

Marcy's tinkling bells ring, "Do you have any idea how much you would earn per hour in California as a psychiatrist? But my lurid confession isn't why I came by this afternoon. I do have some legitimate business."

She gets up again and goes to the liquor cabinet. "Want a brandy?"

"Yes, not whiskey."

She holds up the *Crown Royal* bottle. This is about empty."

"That is the second one. We drank more than I thought."

"I'll have Ben have someone send you replacements from Canada. I know you can't buy it in the US."

"I will fix some coffee. Want me to call Wilson to send

up some sandwiches?"

"No, when we finish, why don't we take supper at the country club? That should give the gossips a new venue."

"You have heard? We tried our best to keep it from you."

"Elton, you are such an innocent; you know nothing about women. Eloise Osborne Cutter is out to settle old and new scores. She was furious when you kept her off the jury; you being her cousin."

"I heard her when you were in Kathryn Burton's court. They intended for you to hear their every word. I could not permit their vitriol to cloud the questions the jury had to address. Why does she hate you?"

"I know. You were doing your job. Elton, my phone is unlisted but I got a call from a 'concerned citizen' with the story of Bill paying me blackmail with the bank's money. Eloise's husband is the manager of the phone company. To answer your other question, she is Cal Osborne's granddaughter and she had Bill staked out as her personal property from the time we were in the tenth grade."

"I do not understand the connection."

"Cal Osborne owned the farm next to Alexander Burton. She dreamed of uniting the two farms when she inherited, but John Henry's father sent him away to military school, which took him out of the picture for her happy-ever-after schemes. Bill became fair game and I stood in her way. Then I made it worse; I bought Cal Osborne's farm."

"You did what? When? I did not prepare a deed for you."

"Part of my business for this afternoon. I bought it the day before I was arrested. Make the coffee, Elton. We have a long afternoon ahead of us."

CHAPTER 26

When I come back with the coffee, she is pacing past my shelves, taking a book down at random, then returning it to its place. Two small cordial glasses are filled, one sits on the coffee table and the other is placed on my desk beside a fresh legal-pad. She wants to keep a distance. There will be no personal talk. I put the tray on the coffee table, pour both of us a cup, using my mother's best French Haviland, and go around to my desk.

It is my desk; my father has been exorcized from the room by her presence. I glance down, a second hundred-dollar bill has been placed in the silver frame. Phillip's has been moved up to make room for both of them.

I look up, but she shakes her head. We both understand its significance. I am bound to the two people I love most in this world both by personal and professional considerations. A bond that will last a lifetime.

"You said you bought Cal Osborne's farm. John Henry bought it at the estate auction. Why did you want it? Your place is in the other direction."

"Elton, for God's sake, don't give me sainthood. I wasn't about to let her get away with what she said when I walked in that courtroom with you. Besides, it's a very sound investment. The back side borders the lake for a thousand feet or more.

"John Henry really didn't want or need it; he just didn't want anyone next to him he didn't know. Buying it before the yearling sales made his cash flow tight, so he was glad to let me have it. His horses are much too valuable to expose to strangers. He'll keep it mowed and use the apples from the orchards for feed. It's a good deal for both of us."

"So now you want me to do a deed of conveyance?"

"Yes, and some other things. You started me thinking when we were talking over Philip's situation. I must add several codicils to my will; I wasn't thinking when I had you prepare it."

She opens her purse and pulls out a thick wad of papers, then puts on her glasses. A tight grin flits across her mouth, "Bifocals. My sight has changed in the last six months, but I have trouble walking when wearing them.

"Now let's see," she hands me a key to a safety deposit-box, "this is a duplicate. I put your name on it so it can be opened before probate, but I want if possible to avoid that procedure. I went through it when Jeremy died. There really isn't much in it, except a few pieces of jewelry I had in my purse the night of the fire. List them in the will as going to Aunt Cynthia as trustee for Kira Lynn."

She studies the papers and checks them against her copy of the will I prepared. This time Marcy has spent a lot of time on her affairs, not like the afternoon she drafted her first will.

"Lend me a pen." She checks off an item on her list, the papers are spread on the low table, the coffee tray pushed to the side. All I can see is the top of her head as she bends over her work.

"You know Cynthia's funds are very limited. She hasn't had any help with expenses since her brother left for the army. She refused help from me. When I was watching families harvest the tobacco crop out by my place, I had this awful feeling I was seeing the end of a way of life. The tobacco poundage has already been cut—I checked at the ASCS office. Delbert Singleton leases her poundage. She can't go on much longer on subsistence farming.

"Elton, make sure she accepts a monthly income from the trust. Bribe her with a threat of telling the truth if you have to, but make her take it. She isn't covered by Social Security, never worked a day in her life outside her home."

"Wait a minute Marcy, you are talking like you are going away."

She goes to the shelf and removes the Bible I keep in the office for reference. It is a small illustrated King James version given to me by my grandmother on my eighth birthday. I keep the leather oiled to retain the supple texture of the cover.

She sits back down and removes her glasses. She holds the Bible in her hands. "This isn't how I planned to tell you, but yes, Elton. Sometime within the next six-months I will go away forever."

"Marcy, I. . . ."

She holds up her right hand. "Remember the century note. Nothing I say must pass these doors. I came home to die. I have cancer and surgery is not an option."

Her statement is blunt and brutal. My heart stops beating. The ugly truth is more than I can endure.

"The only thing I have left is my pride. Elton, I couldn't stay out there in the spotlight and waste away in public."

I start to speak but she interrupts.

"No, don't say anything. Right now I can't tolerate sympathy. Now lets make sure my affairs are in order for my daughter. She is now five and can tell you her name and address. Jeremy taught her if she should ever get lost from us at the zoo. She loves the monkeys."

She wipes her eyes with the back of her hand and puts on her glasses before she lights a cigarette, waving away my attempt to help her.

"These are the names, addresses and phone numbers of everyone in California who is important to me. I have sent yours to them.

"Elroy and Lon have taken on a major responsibility with Tal and Sunny. I told you that day in court I would help. Establish a trust fund for them—use one of those new mutual funds for non-taxable bonds. I've listed the initial amounts, and here are the CD's to cover it. They are payable directly to you on my death because you are listed as joint owner."

"Marcy, these are huge amounts. Can you afford this generosity?"

"Jeremy was an extremely wealthy man. I milked his mother for every cent his stock was worth and then some. She was furious, but she needed his stocks to maintain control of Endicott Pharmaceuticals. I demanded certified cashier's checks in payment. She learned the hard way; the little hillbilly is no dummy. I told you not to believe I am a saint. I was trained in Cynthia Lane's school of business. Then Ben Lehman conducted my finishing course in protecting my assets."

I manage to echo her sparse diction, "You were an excellent student. Have you left anything for me to do?"

"Of course. You get to put all of this on paper in an

acceptable form to avoid as many estate taxes as possible and govern the distribution. I don't envy you—you must go up against some tough characters. You will earn every cent the estate will pay you. I will accept no arguments.

"Which brings me to Elroy and Lon. Set up the same kind of trust for them as for Sunny and Tal." She hands me some more CDs and papers. I do not bother to check the amounts.

"Why Elroy and Lon?"

"Do you remember my room at the farm?"

"The one in the log structure, above the kitchen."

"It had a big fireplace, which wasn't used in the summer. It was also a perfect sound conductor. I would crawl in there and listen to people talk when they came to visit.

"Elroy came back to Brewster County in the summer of 1947; I was ten years old. He and Lon not only pulled me out of that root cellar; he is my father. I've known since hearing them talk while I hid in the fireplace. I have real parents, not two gravestones, but she wouldn't marry him nor let him claim me. She extracted his word of honor that he would respect her wishes, leaving me out in the cold. Elroy doesn't know I am aware of his part in my life other than as a friend.

"'Shine runners are not covered by Social Security. I have no other way to tell them how much I love them. They are the only true parents I ever had.

"You can read as well as I can." She gathers up the remains of her notes and dumps them on my desk. "Fix all of this in proper form and we'll sign everything before Judge Morgan. Maud Tosh is a notary.

"I'm tired of talking; no discussion of what I've said. Maybe later, when I'm not so raw inside.

"Let's go eat. I'm hungry. Then take me home; I'm drunk." She picks up the *Crown Royal* bottle and drops it in the waste can beside my desk. I had not noticed her drinking, but when I carry the coffee pot out to the kitchen, it is still full and stone cold.

Later I stand at the window of my bedroom and watch the large golden Hunter's moon rising in the midnight-blue sky. Philip's father was executed, it was not suicide. A father's rage when he could not protect the daughter he loved from assault, or from rejection by her mother. What a burden you carry Elroy, under the guise of a friendly joke.

I lie down across the big four-poster bed, and for the first time since I was seven years old I cry bitter, hot tears for Marcy, for my lost friends, and for myself.

* * * * *

"Philip, I am so sorry."

"Forget it. The only way I might stand a chance of getting custody of Bill, Jr. is to file a new suit in Brewster County. Silas Morgan's deposition didn't make a dent in public opinion over here. Want to get a cup of coffee before you head home?"

"Yes."

The hearing is a terrible blow to Philip. He has worked so hard to regain custody of his nephew. The Gladen's attorney had tried every avenue available to have the trust fund Philip established moved to Allerton County under the trusteeship of the grandparents.

I presented to the judge all of the legal papers and financial records of the trust, along with a copy of Philip's father's will to establish his right to all the proceeds from the sale of the family home. After the indebtedness to the bank had been paid, it was a small sum.

From his personal funds, Philip endowed the trust for the full amount of the sale. I made sure he owned the trust and that the income would be used only for the child.

Eloise Cutter's vindictive slander against Marcy and Bill was in mind of every person present at the hearing. I sensed it in the stares in our direction during the proceedings. Eloise's vicious revenge has cost Philip his nephew. Somehow, the ugly story of Jobi's illness and her treatment of Bill Jr. has also filtered through the gossip chain. The judge denied him all visiting rights until Bill Jr. reaches fourteen and can choose for himself.

There are too many family connections between the two counties to unravel the bonds that tie Philip's hands. His maternal family has abandoned him for their stiff religious beliefs. Sheltering their own greed behind the rigid fundamentalist structure of their church, they condemned Philip just as Cynthia Lane's refusal to acknowledge her own child to protect her standing in the community had condemned Marcy.

"What do you want me to do?"

"Look, I was thinking on the way over here. Bill Jr. has suffered enough. He has lost his father. Mine wasn't much, but he was there for me. The boy will never know that security. I don't want to put him through any more in-fighting. We know all they want is the money. Did you see their faces?"

"Rather stern, reminded me of my father or Reverend Haskins."

"You're right there. They're dyed-in-the-wool Bible-thumpers. Hell and damnation is their abiding creed. Poor kid."

"Oh, dear."

"You'll do a good job with the money but get receipts for every cent they spend. I want to make sure it's going to him.

"How is Dan coming with discovering who killed Bill and Jobi?"

Philip continues to dump sugar in the sour coffee. Terrible brew; it tastes as though it has been sitting on the burner all morning. During the months since the fire he has lost the gaunt look he wore for so long. His coffee must be syrup by now but he only takes a small sip.

"Dan is frustrated. He has been unable to move beyond the scenario of Marcy's diagrams."

"I miss her. She doesn't come riding like she did. I guess I'd hoped that if Dan could find the real killer then maybe I'd have a chance to at least see Little Bill play football or something when he gets in school, or maybe teach him, to ride. I could get him a pony."

"You said 'who' killed Bill and Jobi. Do you think that they were murdered by the same person?"

"Only idea that makes sense."

"I believe you are correct, but nothing will be resolved until we know why they were murdered. Keep that thought in mind, it may change everything when Dan learns the truth. He will never stop looking until he does."

CHAPTER 27

Beckworth is laying piles of records on his massive work table as I enter his office. Dan Sommers is standing by the open window looking between the bars into the small courtyard at the white oak. Maybe he is remembering the many times he'd climbed it as a boy.

Beckworth had a wall of river rock constructed from the back of the bank to the alley in order to protect the single tree that remains from the forests of our ancestors. No longer is it a haven where small children can dream dreams amid the grandeur of its massive limbs. He deemed it a safety hazard and wanted it cut down but bowed to the protests of the board.

His office is like the tree, crammed within four walls. I have to work to keep a smile off my face as I wonder if he had to take the legs off to get the table through the door. He takes the single outside chair, and motions for us to sit, with our backs to the window. Dan pulls a chair out as far as possible so I can squeeze my legs under the table.

I hated the thing when it was in my grandmother's

dining room, I was always placed where my legs were wrapped around one of the huge legs. Father maintained it kept me from fidgeting. Life has not changed; I have to maneuver to get the support post between them or sit sideways in the chair.

Beckworth opens the meeting in an abrupt fashion, with no word of greeting. "The other board members are either out of town or couldn't make it at the last minute. It doesn't matter, the State only requires two signatures on their audit, the treasurer and president of the board. You're both present so we will proceed.

"I can't tell you how shocked the staff of the bank has been with the perfidy of Bill Leighton. He was a trusted employee. Help yourself to a sandwich and coffee."

He pushes two cups and a thermos across the table, and follows it with a tray. The milk has been skimmed of cream.

Dan lifts the paper napkin from the sandwiches with a look of dismay. Edges are curled and dry while watery pimento cheese runs down the sides, others are soggy. The rank odor of tuna fish hits me in the face. He drops the napkin and pushes the plate to the side. The smell remains.

"My secretary fixed them, we are cutting expenses to meet the state requirements."

I fill my cup with coffee; Dan spoons sugar into his cup before he tops it off with coffee. The coffee is tepid and tastes as if it is left over from yesterday. I envy Dan his sugar. Miss Feishter would feed her cat the remains of the tuna. At least his would be fresh and not sitting out all afternoon; she leaves at twelve.

Dan and I, both jump, spilling our coffee, as a loud crash resounds from outside the office. Metal banging against metal, clinging and clanking like a gong going off.

Beckworth does not move, but continues to sort papers.

"What was that?" Dan looks at Beckworth.

"Here, use the towel over the sandwiches to mop up your coffee. Vern Osborne, cleaned out his horse racing machine today. The clamor is his deposit through the night window. It's enough to wake the dead if you've never heard it before. You'd think those rubber-lined bags would muffle some of the dim."

We soak up the mess and Beckworth takes the soggy towel over to a waste can behind his desk. I am grateful we no longer have to pretend to drink the foul brew. Dan confirms his feeling with a sly wink.

"Rubber-lined?" I watch Dan's interest focus on the money bags.

"Before your time. Some kids dumped water through the depository slot, ruined the payroll checks from the papermill. The board authorized special waterproof deposit bags.

"We're getting side-tracked by Vern's deposit. It's getting late, my wife is waiting dinner. Let's take care of this nasty business then I can deliver these papers to Capital City in the morning. It has been an ugly business and I'm glad to see it behind us.

"I've cut expenses enough to continue to serve the needs of our customers. Sign where I've marked."

He pushes a stack of papers toward us, and as he does, a tiny shaft of dying afternoon sun breaks through an opening in the leaves of the tree. It strikes his gold cuff link reflecting across the surface of the table.

Dan begins to read.

"That's not necessary. They're all in order."

"Humor me, Cadel. Office habit, I read everything before I sign anything."

As Beckworth runs his right hand through his hair in disgust, his left hand sweeps above the piles, and once again the cuff link glitters for a moment, reminding me of something.

"Every detail isn't important. If you read all this, we'll be here most of the night."

Dan leans back in his chair, purposely taking the top page which he carefully reads before passing it over to me, not looking my way. The page is the new hours for the bank: open at ten, close at noon, then reopen at one till three, five days a week. There will be different tellers for each two hour shift, Miss Feishter will be on duty for the morning shift, while Beckworth retains full employment as president.

I reread the paper to make sure I haven't misread his plans. "What is the bank paying the employees?"

"What we've always paid, the minimum wage."

"What is the current minimum wage?"

"Dollar and thirty cents an hour."

"Cadel, with this schedule Calvin Forkes will take home thirteen dollars a week. He has a home and a wife; they cannot live on that amount."

No wonder Bill had to borrow ten dollars from Philip until payday. Even on a full salary, with the way Jobi bought clothes and kept redecorating that house, it is difficult to see how they had enough money to buy groceries. I had no idea.

"Elton, it's worse."

"How?"

"Social Security and income taxes are deducted so take home-pay is less than salary earned. I just did some figuring, the bank is proposing paying their employees six hundred seventy-six dollars a year. That is less than people made during the depression. All Calvin Forkes has to do is go over to Buckston to the bank. They'll be glad to have him. First Farmer's will lose a skilled and valuable employee. Mr. Beckworth, as treasurer, I find this unacceptable."

"Sheriff, I am following the guidelines Mr. Stolmeyer laid out for the restitution of the money Bill Leighton stole. The total sum comes to over thirty thousand dollars."

He keeps referring to Bill as the thief, but Philip is positive Bill would not have taken a dime that did not belong to him.

"What evidence do you have that Mr. Leighton was the thief?"

"Sheriff, customers were paid their standard dividends after he was killed. The audit showed the thefts began shortly after he became an officer and stopped after his death. It seems evident to me. . . ."

Dan holds up a several sheets of paper. "These are audit reports by the examiner's office and they state they can find no evidence of any mal—malfeasance on the part of Mr. William Leighton."

"Where did you get that?" Beckworth almost yells at Dan.

"It was in this stack of papers you asked us to sign or initial without reading."

Beckworth reaches for the papers as if to snatch them from Dan.

"Dan, let me see those papers. I am not an accountant, but I can read a financial statement. We need to work out an equitable settlement for all parties concerned and that includes the employees of the bank.

"Mr. Beckworth, maybe you had best phone your wife that you will be late for supper."

191

I start reading the state report. Bill Leighton's account showed the same expenditures month after month: groceries, utilities, a car payment, etc. Normal expenses for a household. The only deposit in seven years outside his paycheck was a small inheritance from his father, which was dispersed to Clark's for funeral expenses. The state's conclusion was that Mr. Leighton's accounts showed no evidence of embezzlement.

Philip was astute in his assessment of Bill's honesty. Philip said the last words Bill said to him were, "I've got to right a wrong that has existed for a long time."

"Dan, can you find reports like this on the other employees?"

"No, I've been looking while you read Bill's. There is nothing here. Cadel, were audits completed on Calvin Forkes, Miss Feishter and yourself?"

"Yes, I'm sure they were, but a person's financial records are a private matter. Please accept my apologies, Mr. Leighton's audit should not have been mixed up with the proposals to insure the bank's responsibility to its customers and maintain solvency. It was an error on Miss Feishter's part when she prepared our evening's agenda."

He keeps twisting a ring around his finger as he answers our questions.

"We understand the need for privacy, but as trustees for First Farmers our first responsibility is to the citizens who intrust us with their financial security. The audit of William Leighton's account clearly demonstrates he was not at fault, yet he still stands accused by you of being the perpetrator of the fraud. His name must be cleared and not left to innuendo or conjecture."

Beckworth gets up and goes over to his desk to call his wife. "Gentlemen, we are getting side-tracked. As members of the board of trustees it is your duty to expedite those proposals so the bank can continue in operation during this difficult period of transition. Everyone must make sacrifices to insure the best service for the bank's customers."

Oh dear, I am glad Philip is not here. What did he call Beckworth, a pompous so-and-so? I cannot remember his exact words but they were not complementary.

He sounds like he is talking to a luncheon group, nothing but hot air. "Mr. Beckworth, we are doing just as you have delegated, but in good-faith neither Sheriff Sommers nor I can sign any papers for the board until we have read them.

"Now I suggest you sit down with us and we will work out a plan for repayment that will not cost the bank the services of its most experienced teller. Calvin Forkes has worked here since I was a child. In many respects, to the community, he *is* the bank."

I can be as long-winded as Beckworth but the man is furious because we will not rubber-stamp his plans. He runs his hand though his hair a second time causing it to stick up in clumps. A sunray hits his cufflink.

No, his ring—he is wearing a horseshoe-shaped ring on his left-hand set with diamonds!

"Beckworth. . . ."

"You killed Bill Leighton." Dan's accusation thunders in the air.

He turns, pointing a black pistol at us.

"Gentlemen, do not move. No, Sheriff, I will kill Fightmaster if you try to play hero. Leave your hands on the table and stay in your seats."

His eyes lock with mine. He is not sure how we made the correct connections to the puzzle, but Dan's words echo around the silent room. He comes around the desk and backs toward the door.

"You'll never get away with it." Dan starts to move, straining with his stomach against the old table. It does not move.

I stare at the dark round hole of the barrel pointed directly at me, it seems to get larger and larger as he backs away toward the door. I try to move my right leg behind the post of the table to help Dan, but my chair is against the wall.

"You're to sit there until I leave." He holds the keys in his left hand. "It will take a while for someone to rescue you. The windows are barred and everyone has gone home for supper. Besides, Fightmaster can't climb trees. He sniggers, a rough nervous laugh, and backs through the door.

"Sorry I don't have the time to stay around and discuss your reasoning. But I prepared for emergencies."

He begins to close the door with his left hand, the key ring dangling from his thumb.

Dan slams me down against the table and fires three rapid shots.

Thick gun smoke clouds my vision, acrid and sharp, mingling with Beckworth's cigar smoke, which is smoldering in the ash tray by my nose. My ears reverberate with the peal of the wailing of the courthouse siren.

I hear a slight groan, and a gasp, "Don't think he hit anything vital. Can't move my arm. Help me."

I get my nose out of the stinking ashtray. Dan is slumped in his chair, holding his shoulder. Blood is spurting through his fingers.

"See about him. I'll hold. Can't feel. . .call Doc. . . ."

I am going to make a bonfire with this damn table. I

finally make it out and cross the room to the telephone on Beckworth's desk. It is dead, the cord is lying on the floor.

Pounding, someone is pounding on the front door. Beckworth blocks the door. I have to move him so I can get through. Then I fumble with the unfamiliar locks, wasting more time with my clumsiness.

"What happened? We heard shots."

"Dan—Dan in the office!"

Elroy and Lon rush past me, ignoring Beckworth. By the time I make it back to the office, they have Dan spread out on the table.

"The bastard nicked an artery. Call Doc Flanders. Tell him to hurry. Lon's trying to hold it together."

I find a phone on Calvin Forkes' desk and make the call. My hands are shaking so badly I can barely move the dial. Mr. Forkes, with his usual efficiency, has a list of emergency phone numbers taped under the receiver.

"He is on his way with the ambulance."

I point, I do not have the strength to talk, my teeth start to chatter.

"Him? He's dead." How can Lon be so matter-of-fact? "Bled a lot, odd—you wouldn't think he had that much in him."

The idea that Lon's response is Shakespearean floats though my mind in a vague daze, irrelevant and absurd.

The siren shuts down as Doc Flanders bolts through the front door, which, in my frantic concern for Dan, I left standing wide open.

Elroy meets me at the door to Beckworth's office, "Sit down, Elton. You look a little peaked."

"Dan?"

"Lon's thumb is stoppin' his leaking artery. Were you hit?"

"Of course not."

"Must be Dan's blood on your coat."

"Oh dear." I sit on the edge of Forkes' desk before I make a fool of myself and fall down.

"Elroy, help me get Dan on the stretcher."

They carry Dan out the door as I move out of their way. Lon is walking beside the stretcher holding his fingers to Dan's neck.

"Lon goes with us. When we get Dan loaded," Doc Flanders nods at me, "come back and take him home. He's in shock, and I don't need two patients on my hands.

"While you're at Elton's call Wilson. Tell him to make some biscuits and fry up some of those sausages he gives Betsy Duncan. Bring them to the hospital, it's going to be a long night."

CHAPTER 28

N o, Wilson. Coffee is all I can take right now." I almost did not make it up the stairs after Elroy insisted on pouring brandy down my throat. All night long I kept seeing Dan's blood pumping through his fingers.

"Doc Flanders said no visitors until after lunch. Dan is doing as well as expected. He wants him to sleep as long as possible. What happened last night? What little I saw through the windows at the bank. It looked like the shootout at the OK Corral." Tom exaggerates.

"I know. I called the hospital the first thing this morning."

The backdoor bangs. "Elroy said Lon had to give blood for Dan. Beckworth shot him. Does Dan need more blood?"

"No need. Dan is coming along."

"Doctor Flanders refused to allow me to see the sheriff. The bank is a disaster. There is blood all over the table in Beckworth's office, his papers are ruined, blood in the doorway, and the front door was unlocked. I walked right in. I was told Beckworth is dead, shot by Sheriff Sommers."

"Sit down, Harrington, here's Elton's breakfast. He won't eat it. No sense in it going to waste."

Harrington starts to sit in Dan's chair but stern looks stop him. He takes a chair on the far side of Marcy where Philip sits.

"Where's Philip?"

"I would presume he's sleeping it off. He was really tying one on at the country club last night. The manager asked him to leave."

"Oh dear."

"Don't worry about the lush; he was feeling no pain. What happened last night? Has Sommers lost his mind, killing the bank president?"

Before I can say a word, Marcy rounds on him like a forest fire.

"Listen you dissected worm. If you say one more disparaging word, I will empty that plate over your hollow head."

He is so shocked, his mouth opens. Her hands fly—she opens a biscuit, inserts a sausage and crams it in his mouth. "Make the only legitimate use of that trap you can." She turns back to me, leaving Harrington choking.

"Elton, what did happen last night? Elroy said you were there."

"Doc didn't mention you."

Through his mouthful of crumbs I hear, "Fitmuster as ere. I'm thu office of thu cort."

Elroy and Lon come through from the kitchen carrying plates, followed by Wilson with two more plates and a full coffee pot. He puts one down in front of me and another at the end of the table, then walks over to the door.

"Eat it and no arguments." He flips the lock, turns the sign to closed and pulls the shades. "Now we will not be disturbed by gawkers. What did happen last night?"

"Tell us Elton, we only got in on the KP duty. Dan sure leaves a mess when he cleans up Sodom and Gomorrah."

"Marcy gal, pass Gilbert the coffee; he's havin' trouble swallowin'."

She picks up the tall red Fiesta pot. Green eyes meet green eyes.

"No, that isn't nice. In his cup." She has the audacity to stick out her bottom lip and pout.

Tom Clement pushes his plate to the side and gets out his pad and pencil. "I was coming back from taking Betty and Aaron out to dinner. We followed the ambulance to the hospital. Doc brushed me off, said to call this morning.

"I hung around until Elroy and Wilson arrived with food but they couldn't tell me anything. When we got back, your lights were out. As I told you, Doc did not mention your presence." He smooths his mustache and licks the end of the pencil, while refilling his coffee cup.

"Start at the beginning. This is an official interview for the paper."

"Tom, I cannot give you an interview for the paper."

His gray eyes bore into mine. "Then give me the facts for Dan's report; I'll get his permission as to what to put in the paper this afternoon. Quit stalling."

I have no choice. I tell them what I remember.

"You mean he killed Jobi to keep her from identifying him as Bill's killer?"

"I believe so. Remember, Father Bryan or Ben Lehman said he left the witness room on Monday, while court was in session."

"Vaguely. We were all talking."

"Gilbert, did you lock the bank?"

"Yes, I met Calvin Forkes on the steps and sent him home."

"Good. The bank is a crime scene. Dan will have to go

over it before business can resume and then it will need to be cleaned.

"I'll call Buckston National as the president of the board and request they handle First Farmer's business for the next few days. It means an inconvenience to the customers but I don't know what else to do until I talk to Dan."

"What do you mean a crime scene? Last night was straight forward. Beckworth shot Sheriff Sommers and Sommers killed him."

"I'm talking about when Bill was killed. I believe he was killed in Beckworth's office."

"Are you sure? He was very upset when we found Leighton's corpse on the golf course."

"Harrington, he was an actor, a magnificent actor. Dan and I refused to sign the reorganization of the bank papers and he panicked. Last night, he was prepared to kill both of us, even before he realized we had discovered the truth.

"Beckworth, himself, told us about the rubber lined money bags when Vern Osborne used the night depository."

"So."

"Remember what the state coroner said at the trial. He mentioned he thought Bill's head was beaten while inside a covering that left little fleck of a rubber-like material in his skull. Beckworth wasn't present during the testimony and did not know about the report. "

"Oh!"

"You were too busy trying to railroad me to pay any attention. . . ."

"Marcy gal, that's over and done with. Keep quite and let Elton tell us what happened."

I take a sip of my cold coffee; I am not used to talking so much. "Calvin Forkes' desk was piled with those bags the last time I was in the bank.

"Beckworth's office had been rearranged. A new rug was put down over the old carpeting. I saw the changes when Stolmeyer was here. The room smelt to high heaven. I assumed the odor was carpet-fumes from where the new one covered the heat vents. But, after last night, I believe it was blood. I could smell Dan's blood over Beckworth's cigar. It is an odor you will never forget."

Tom nods but does not lookup. The silence in the Kricket is so acute my voice seems to echo.

"Bill's car was parked by the bank the entire night of the fire. Dan never found his keys. Here I am guessing but I think Jobi took them from the car and used them to let herself into the bank. Her last words were, 'I saw you through the door.' It is the only scenario that makes sense."

"Is Cadel's body still in the bank?"

"I do not. . . ."

"No. When we came back through town, Clark was picking it up. Doc sent the ambulance back for the remains."

"Lon, I was never so thankful when I opened the front door to you and Elroy. I had no idea how to help Dan. I was never so scared in my life as when I looked down the barrel of that gun."

"Period and a report." Tom smooths his mustache, closes the notebook and plunges the pencil into his breast pocket.

Elroy grins. "I heard a new Clem story.

"Clem was visitin' the barber shop when Tom Clement came in sportin' a new black mustache.

"'Hey Tom, what are you usin' on the mouth-mop, shoe polish?'

"'Nah. My wife's mascara, it's waterproof.'"

"Blasphemy! Making fun of my mustache is a criminal offense. I must send Father Stanley a new supply of candles. Are there any black candles left over from Halloween?"

CHAPTER 29

Silence is playing at Cloverton. Will you go to the movies with me?"

"Elton, you mean, like a real date to the cinema?"

"I could never ask you when we were in high school. I did not have a car. Consider it making up for lost time. The whole works, dinner at the Kricket, the movies, then we will find a place to stop for a soda."

"I'd love to, except please, take me to the country club. If we eat at the Kricket, we'll end up with three chaperones." Marcy giggles.

"Fine I'll pick you up about five. Want me to blow the horn?"

"Mr. Fightmaster, you will come to the front door like a proper young squire. I'm not a cheap pickup; I haven't eaten since breakfast." She giggles again and hangs up the phone.

Marcy's gay mood is infectious. I know she has days when she is in dire pain and all her strength pours out of her, but today has obviously been a good one.

I have a real date with the only girl I have ever loved.

Our very first and maybe our last. I glance at the calendar on my desk. Thanksgiving is next week. Time is running out for her. She has forbidden me to mention what is happening and remembering the many times she waited for me to get my feet under me, I respect her wishes.

* * * * *

"I couldn't believe that was me on the screen. I've never seen a completed film."

"You attended the premiers."

"But I've never watched one of my films; I couldn't. I hid in the bathroom during the showings. I was always afraid they would be a bomb."

"Unsure of your talent?"

"Have you got a cigarette?"

I take my hand off the wheel and hand her a pack of Viceroys. I keep them for her, even though she stopped smoking sometime back.

She punches in the lighter. "No, I'll light it, you watch your driving. Did you ever wonder why you are living at this time in this place?"

She has the incredible habit of changing the subject when you least expect it.

I have to be honest with her. "No, but I am grateful for the privilege. I try to get through the days without giving in—I must fight every day to not end up a complete cripple. It does not leave much time for deep introspection. Marcy, I gave up on religion a long time ago."

"I know, I've always known. Right now it's all I have to hold on to. I've been reading your Bible and it does help. Seeing *Silence* tonight made me remember how miserable I was when it was filmed. I thought Kira Lynn would be born deformed from the corsets I had to wear."

"Ben Lehman told me about how the director hid your pregnancy. He also said your discomfort gave your character a depth that led to your Oscar nomination."

"Ben said that. How sweet. I was thinking of Kira Lynn the entire time I watched the film."

"Marcy, she will be found. Do you remember Clayton Forrester? He was a senior when we were freshmen."

"Of course. The sexiest guy I ever knew. He didn't pay much attention to us; we were children to the upperclassmen. But I sensed he was dangerous. Danger in a man is like a magnet to a woman. It's there, no matter what age you are. Now you know all my dark secrets. Why did you ask if I remembered him?"

"He lives in California. I called him some weeks ago to ask him to search for your daughter. So far he has not had much luck, going over the same paths your detectives followed, but he is going to keep looking. Now don't get your hopes up, but he believes your mother-in-law knows exactly where your daughter is located."

Her hands grip my leg, "Elton! I've always thought the same thing. Where else would Jeremy have taken her? I got a court order for a house search and nothing turned up. He will keep looking?"

"Yes. He gave me his word."

"Elton, I was an orphan all my life. I have a mother who doesn't recognize me or allow my father to. All of her life my daughter will be an orphan. You must find her and let her know how much I love her. I have nothing else of real value to give her."

"Marcy, your talent is your greatest gift. The pleasure you give to the world—the films you leave behind for your daughter to know you."

She slips her hand in mine. "Thank you, my friend, for reminding me of my work. I did make a contribution."

I hold her hand all the way to her door.

* * * * *

I hate hospital rooms; I have spent so much of my life in them. Tom called to say Dan insisted on seeing me this afternoon.

Dan is lying in a bed that seems too small for his large frame and fussing with the bandage around his neck and shoulder. A clear solution runs from an IV drip into his arm, probably glucose or saline.

"Come on in, hang the no visitors-sign on the knob and shut the door."

"You sound stronger than I have been led to believe. Doc's been rather touchy about allowing visitors."

"Opal put him up to it. She isn't happy about the other night but she's gone home to let the dog out. This is worse than a tie and I hate ties." He pulls at the bandage.

"I know I've got to see Harrington but I wanted to check your story first. Did Tom leave anything out of his notes?"

"Have you ever known Mr. Meticulous to miss a detail?"

"He didn't mention these." Dan reaches in the drawer of his meal tray table and hands me two bullets.

"Doc dug the small one out of my shoulder. Clark got the big one out of Beckworth. How many gun shots did you hear?"

"I am not sure but I thought there were three. I forgot to say anything about it."

"Good. Look at my holster hanging on the back of the bed."

"The leather is burned at the bottom, how did you do that?"

"Elton, if you look, I'll swear the bullet from my gun went into the leg of that big table. Doc pulled some splinters out of the back of my hand. I shot before I pulled my gun, probably when I took the hit. I didn't shoot Beckworth, that's for damn sure."

"Things were happening so fast, you pushed me down against the table, Beckworth shot you. How do you know you did not shoot him?"

"You told me you don't know anything about guns. The bullet Clark dug out of Beckworth. It's a forty-five; my service revolver is a thirty-eight, the same caliber as the gun Beckworth used to shoot me."

"Oh dear." Philip's voice rings in my mind. Raymond Clark dug a forty-five caliber bullet out of Beckworth, the same size bullet his father had buried with Philip's father.

"Oh dear is right. Where did you get such a silly expression?"

"Soap mouthwash when I was about four. I heard my grandmother use an exciting new word and I used it."

"Been there. Didn't mean to get off track. I laughed when Tom read me the part about my pushing you down to the table. I didn't correct him, no point."

"What was so funny?"

" It was impossible. I was sitting to the left of you. How could I have pushed you to the table and pulled my gun at the same time, while taking a bullet in my left shoulder. I'm right-handed."

I stand by his bed, moving my right arm. Trying to push down and reach for a gun at the same time. Then clutch my left shoulder.

"Doesn't work does it?"

I am sure I look sheepish. "No. But what did happen?"

"Thank your lucky stars, this is one case that will never go to court. You aren't a good witness."

"Witness! I was terrified when he pointed that gun at me."

"There were three shots, true, but you were already down on the table because someone got you out of the way through that open window. Then they shot Beckworth over your body. I've spent most of the day when Opal thought I was sleeping figuring it out."

"To whom do we owe our lives?"

"Have no idea and I don't care to know. That is one can-of-worms I will never open. What were you thinking about when you said Beckworth's name just before the shooting started?"

"The money bags and his ring."

"His ring?"

"He was wearing a horseshoe ring set with diamonds, the sun caught it when he ran his hand through his hair. It was the same flash I saw before Jobi went out the window."

"Of course; I saw it, too, but it didn't register. The only detail that was different in the descriptions. I've got to get out of here."

"Wait a minute, you are not able to get out of bed."

"Of course I am. Lon's blood is working just fine. I've been avoiding Harrington. Can't play-act now. . .got too much work to do."

"What do you need?"

"Have to get my bullet out of the table."

"Is it needed for evidence, the table I mean?"

"Only thing of value it has on it is my blood."

"Then I will do what I wanted to do the other night.

Burn the damn thing. It was my grandmother's dining room table. I hated sitting with my legs around those big posts then, and Monday night did not restore it to my favor."

"Good. Are we talking as sheriff to civilian or bank board president and treasurer."

"Bank board. The table becomes a bonfire. We have work to do in that capacity."

"I nominate Calvin Forkes as the new president."

"We are thinking alike. It must be presented to the full board in a formal session. Beckworth lied to us. I called the other board members this morning—he had not notified them of an emergency meeting."

"He intended to use us because we are new to the board."

"His fatal error. He did not consider that we would balk about signing those papers before we read them."

"Oh, yes, while we are in session, find a stone mason to make a gate in that damn wall. All children should have trees to climb, trees that were here when the Indians walked the land."

"I will do it and I will have some benches put under it for dreaming."

"I'll get Opal to run me by the bank tomorrow as Sheriff to finish my investigation. Get someone to take up that carpet and move those filing cabinets. Don't think I'll be up to that. One more thing, get that ring of keys out of the drawer."

He is trying to point to the little cabinet on top of the bedside table. "I see it, stop that! You could pull something!"

The keys are on a fancy ring, and one of them is to a safety-deposit box.

"These Beckworth's?"

"Yes, Clark brought them when he brought the bullets. Find out what they fit."

"What about these?"

"Elton, how many bullets are you holding in your hand?"

"Two."

"Give them back to me. They weren't a gift from the Trojans."

* * * * *

Philip refuses to visit Marcy. He is ashamed to admit he has fallen off the wagon but she insisted I bring him out to her home. I did nothing less than kidnap him, because he must make his own peace with her.

Today is warm for December and she waves from the porch as we drive in her lane. When we get out of the car, I have to push Philip up to the porch. He is not sober, but well enough.

She won't give in to going to bed. She is sitting on her porch in a rocking chair with a long belt though the spokes to help to hold her upright and save her pride. My grandmother's afghan covers her legs. Her fiery hair, glowing in the sun, seems too heavy for her shrunken body. Dark shadows under her eyes are almost black beneath thick makeup. My arms ache to pull her to me and hold her safe against the coming night.

I watch Philip's face. He is shocked at the change in Marcy. He hangs his head. I turn away to give him privacy for the tears I see on his face.

To give him time to recover, I put an idea to Marcy I have been turning over in my mind for days.

"What do you think of Philip's becoming a member of

the board at First Farmers?"

"Me? Why are you asking me?"

"You are one of the major depositors." I can tell Philip is listening hard as he stares out toward the road.

She looks at me and knows what I am trying to do. "Is he qualified, with the bank involved in the fraud problem?"

"He *solved* the problem."

"How?"

"The missing money never left the bank. Beckworth had a safety deposit box."

"It was full of cash."

"No, certificates of deposit. He'd issue one to himself each time he shorted the passbook accounts, then write a new one combining several when the maturity dates came around for the face value and accumulated interest. All the records were there but in different files. Philip traced the transactions. He knows money like you do."

"Then he's the man for the job. He has my vote with the provision he get off the sauce."

Philip turns around to face us, "I don't want the job."

"Yes, you do. It is just the thing to make people forget all of your work at trying to become the town lush. Kyle Lefter holds that dubious honor. Don't be a fool. Don't be afraid to forget. Remembering is a luxury you can no longer afford."

"Marcy, I can't handle. . . ."

Marcy is past kindness. She dives right into him.

"You lost Bill's son and I lost my daughter. Hiding will not bring them back. I can't change Eloise Cutter's vicious gossip. I know her ugly mouth hurt you."

"You will be vindicated when no one cares. Yesterdays are of no importance—all her anger and chagrin are less than pebbles."

"Elton, I warned you about platitudes. Shut up and stay out of this."

"Marcy, he was only trying to help."

"I know what he is trying to do. Now you listen to me. You are afraid to forget. Phillip, you weren't responsible for what your father did to me."

"But, Marcy. . . ."

"Don't but Marcy, me, I watched you ride that horse. The demons are gone. Between us we've filled a cemetery with them. You did so well when Jobi died and you had Bill Jr. to consider. Stop behaving like a child.

"Children are self-centered creatures. The world revolves around us, but we haven't been young for a long time. You only grow up when you realize you aren't the center of the universe, other people inhabit the world. You haven't been sober since your parents died. I've lived in tinsel land. It isn't real for either of us."

"Marcy, I. . . ."

"Yes, you can. Clean out from under the sink or wherever you keep your stash. Elton, make sure that he does. Take whatever wonderful largess the world gives you and hold on. Friendships based on trust last for your lifetime. They're precious, but never what we imagine they're going to be."

"I don't know if. . . ."

"Don't give me that hogwash. Of course you can. Promise that you will, your word of honor. It's all I ask of you."

Philip is gripping the porch post. "You know I can't deny you anything."

"Good. You have the rest of your life to keep it. It is getting chilly out here with the sun going down. Elton, you must give me your arm. I need help getting to the kitchen.

Philip is going to start right now.

"I've made coffee."

* * * * *

I eased the phone back on the cradle. I knew it was coming but Elroy's call caught me by surprise. I am numb. I have known pain, but never the kind that wrenches my heart out of my chest and holds it up, dripping before my eyes. The earth's rotation was not fast enough for her blithe spirit.

I find the pack of Viceroys I have carried in my pocket and light one before I open the middle drawer of my desk to remove the packet Marcy had handed me as Philip and I left her last week. She winked at me and lifted her coffee cup in a salute, the one Wilson had given her to use at the Kricket with a gold star. It was the last time I saw her.

I turn it over to open it. Across the flap she has written, "I'm adding one more burden for you to carry on your strong shoulders, Do not let him forget his promise."

A letter is wrapped around some heavy paper. I read her final instructions through my tears.

Elton, my dearest friend. I wish to be buried beside my family under my own name. Please make sure my casket is closed and the service private. Do not under any circumstance let Tom print an obituary.

I told you I am not a saint. Priscilla Ann van Ledmeir Endicott took my baby and for this she will pay the rest of her life. She is never to be informed of my demise. This letter is accompanied by the stock certificates I withheld from the sale-controlling interest of Endicott Pharmaceuticals with full voting rights made out to you to be transferred to Kira Lynn or your heir.

By now she knows the "gutter-snipe" (where did she get that label? Vassar or Dickens?) tricked her. She has agents combing the country looking for me. Tell Clayton to be very careful to give her no information or trace of me. I want her to live every day of the rest of her life wondering when I will come out of the woodwork. I may be unable to get even but I will have my revenge.

Our date was so special. I've recorded every moment in my heart for always.

Marcy

* * * * *

Dan Sommers blocks the drive to Cynthia Lane's home with his cruiser once we are inside the gate. When we emerge from our cars a sharp wind off the lake cuts through our clothes like a knife. The sky is a bright, clear blue, unusual for a winter day. At least it is not raining as it has for so many funerals I have attended.

We walk up the drive. Each step carefully placed on the uneven gravel so I can maintain my balance. Phillip is in rough shape, I can see his tremors against the steel of her coffin but he hasn't touched a drop since he gave his promise.

Wilson, Tom, Philip, Lon, Elroy, and Gilbert Harrington carry the white casket to the open grave and place it on the bier. Banks of white roses cover the sod.

Dan and I follow Monsignor Stanley and Ben Lehman in the small processional. Harrington is filling in for Dan as a pallbearer because Dan's arm is in a sling. He was admitted to our group this morning by Wilson, who presented him with his official cup—marked with a lighted bulb covered by a pair of thick lensed glasses. Wilson has a kind heart and felt sorry for Harrington, sitting alone.

The rack now has a white shelf above it, with one lone

cup bearing a gold star.

Only those who truly loved her are present to see her home. Raymond Clark hands me my cane and walks back with Harrington to stand by the hearse.

Marcy converted to Catholicism to marry her husband but in her last months reverted to the faith of her childhood. She has returned to the land of her ancestors to rest in peace.

I look toward the house, Cynthia Lane is standing on the porch watching with her arms crossed across her chest, her face stiff with indignation. I had to follow Marcy's instructions to get her to assent to the burial in the family cemetery.

Elroy and Lon mount the steps and take Miss Cynthia's arms to force her to walk with them to see their daughter home. She resists, but Elroy, his pleasant face savage and grim with lines of determination, says something to her and she places her hand on his arm. He pulls it under his arm and places his right hand over hers.

Lon performs the same action on her left. Her face remains stern after losing the argument, but they walk to the open grave with great ceremony.

The four friends wear the same suits they wore the day they appeared in court. I now recognize one of the ribbon bars on their coats—all of these men received the Purple Heart for bravery above and beyond the call of duty. Wilson wears the same bar as a lapel pin.

Southern Baptist Margery Lynn Lane is laid to rest beside Thomas Osborne Lane and Mollie Burton while her real parents watch as the simple service is performed by a Jewish rabbi and a Catholic priest.

Venus, the evening star, glorious and beautiful, blazes alone in the western sky as the last shovel of soil covers her.

ACKNOWLEDGEMENTS

Thank you to:

Phil Sullivan, a retired banker who taught us how to commit bank fraud and the other bankers who backed our financial decisions, Fred Nicholas, Carrick James, Jack Lancaster, Zack Sofley, Bill Jennings and Gaylon Neat.

Chris, Mildred, Fil, Tene, Jan and Glenna, the staff of the Russell County Public Library, who make our work so much easier.

Charles Fought of Homestead Computers who keeps ours going when gremlins strike.

Pat Lobrutto, for urging us to keep writing on this volume when the story got rough and life equaled fiction.

Clyde Davenport, *Pounchion Camps*, Monticello, KY, recorded by the Appalachian Center, Berea, KY, for the fiddle and banjo tunes of the Cumberland Mountains, winner of the 1992 National Heritage Award.

Mary Lena Berdet, editor and Michele Center, OutSkirts Press who handled the detail work.

All mistakes are the responsibility of the authors.

NOTES

This volume of the Brewster County series took seven years to write. We wanted to illustrate, through the character of Jobi Leighton, the disintegration of a human personality when subjected to child molestation. The subject was carefully researched through standard academic channels over a period of years before the actual writing began.

While writing we became involved with the Lake Cumberland Children's Advocacy Center as members of a ten-county regional team working to create a sanctuary where abused children could be examined, receive treatment, counseling, and learn the procedures of the court system in a safe environment under one roof.

While building furniture for their child-size courtroom, we met many professionally-skilled dedicated volunteers and a young woman who herself, was a victim of the terror inflicted on those too young to defend themselves. Michaela Jefferies', *Grasping for Love : a child's journey into a loveless world* is raw reality against which mystery/fiction can not be compared.

We rededicate *Sins of the Fathers* to the Lake Cumberland Children's Advocacy Center. One dollar from each sale of this volume will be donated to the Center to help provide adequate funding so no child will scream in the night unheard.

ALSO BY Nash Black

Qualifying Laps - A Brewster County Novel

It was a hot and humid afternoon when ex-race car driver Jim Young and his brother Adam decided to check out Adam's new purchase—the childhood farm where so many memories lay. What the two never expected was to find the car that killed Catherine Throckton with a mummified corpse in the driver's seat. It had been nearly ten years since Catherine was killed by a hit-and-run driver, the same time that a local teenage boy had disappeared. When the eyes of the law turn on Jim, he begins to engage in his own search for answers. But when his brother Adam is savagely attacked by an unknown group of assailants, the Young family bands together to try to solve the decade-old mystery. The more involved they become, the more neighbors keep turning up dead. You'd think the Sheriff of Brewster County would show a little more interest.

Learn more at:
www.outskirtspress.com/qualifyinglaps

ALSO BY Nash Black

Taxes, Stumbling Blocks & Pitfalls for Authors 2007

A clear & concise guide for organizing and preserving expense records for writers as a sole proprietorship under current rules and regulations using Schedule C and its supplements of the 1040 IRS forms. Vital tips for preventing identity theft, keeping your computer free of virus, worm and other headaches, personal security planning and designing worry free book tours. Contains a all 50 states and DC as to their sales tax percentage and contact information.

Learn more at:
www.outskirtspress.com/nashblack

Printed in the United States
96089LV00002B/258/A